"I suppose we'll get married now,"

Michael said.

Bailey's heart beat faster, harder, painfully. "What do you mean?"

"If you're expecting, we'll do the right thing by the child," he said, his tone practical.

Bailey pulled herself up tall, her spine rigid with pride. "The *heck* we will," she declared. "I wouldn't dream of marrying a man who thinks he's going to do the right thing by me. If I was looking to be saved, Michael Wade, I would've married someone else a long time ago."

What a fool I've been. Suddenly she couldn't stay another moment around Michael. Not when it felt like her heart was being torn right out of her.

Dear Reader,

Welcome to another month of wonderful books from Harlequin American Romance! We've rounded up the best stories by your favorite authors, with the hope that you will enjoy reading them as much as we enjoy bringing them to you.

Kick-start a relaxing weekend with the continuation of our fabulous miniseries, THE DADDY CLUB. The hero of Mindy Neff's *A Pregnancy and a Proposal* is one romantic daddy who knows how to sweep a woman off her feet!

Beloved historical author Millie Criswell makes her contemporary romance debut with *The Wedding Planner.* We are thrilled to bring you this compelling story of a wealthy bachelor out to find himself a bride...with a little help from the wedding consultant who wishes she were his only choice!

We've also got the best surprises and secrets. Bailey Dixon has a double surprise for Michael Wade in Tina Leonard's delightful new Western, *Cowboy Be Mine.* And in Bonnie K. Winn's *The Mommy Makeover,* a dedicated career woman is suddenly longing for marriage—what *is* her handsome groom's secret?

With best wishes for happy reading from Harlequin American Romance...

Melissa Jeglinski
Associate Senior Editor

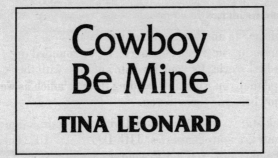

Cowboy Be Mine

TINA LEONARD

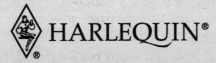

TORONTO • NEW YORK • LONDON
AMSTERDAM • PARIS • SYDNEY • HAMBURG
STOCKHOLM • ATHENS • TOKYO • MILAN • MADRID
PRAGUE • WARSAW • BUDAPEST • AUCKLAND

ISBN 0-373-16811-X

COWBOY BE MINE

Visit us at www.romance.net

Printed in U.S.A.

ABOUT THE AUTHOR

Tina Leonard loves to laugh, which is one of the many reasons she loves writing Harlequin American Romance books. In another lifetime, Tina thought she would be single and an East Coast fashion buyer forever. The unexpected happened when Tina met Tim again after many years—she hadn't seen him since they'd attended school together from first through eighth grade. They married, and now Tina keeps a close eye on her school-age children's friends! Lisa and Dean keep their mother busy with soccer, gymnastics and horseback riding. They are proud of their mom's "kissy books" and eagerly help her any way they can. Tina hopes that readers will enjoy the love of family she writes about in her books. Recently a reviewer wrote, "Leonard has a wonderful sense of the ridiculous," which Tina loved so much, she wants it for her epitaph. Right now, however, she's focusing on her wonderful life and writing a lot more romance!

Books by Tina Leonard

HARLEQUIN AMERICAN ROMANCE
748—COWBOY COOTCHIE-COO
758—DADDY'S LITTLE DARLINGS
771—THE MOST ELIGIBLE…DADDY
796—A MATCH MADE IN TEXAS
811—COWBOY BE MINE

Don't miss any of our special offers. Write to us at the following address for information on our newest releases.

Harlequin Reader Service
U.S.: 3010 Walden Ave., P.O. Box 1325, Buffalo, NY 14269
Canadian: P.O. Box 609, Fort Erie, Ont. L2A 5X3

Chapter One

"I have loved Michael all my life," Bailey Dixon murmured as she stood in her bedroom, staring in the dressing mirror at her full-length profile. "All I ever dreamed of was becoming Mrs. Michael Wade."

She couldn't say that to him. Michael didn't love her. He would be astonished if she just breezed out of her house, drove her truck to his next-door ranch and said, "Michael, it's time you and I—"

What? Put a ring and a commitment on their relationship?

Michael Wade was dead set against rings, commitments and anything that remotely felt like a relationship. A handsome, wealthy bachelor—in Fallen, Texas, he was considered a catch.

Michael Wade would never be caught.

Bailey was terrified of scaring him off. But she would if she mentioned the dreaded M word.

For six months, she had lived in the heaven of his arms—at night. It had happened by accident, almost. He had been under the weather with a broken ankle. Knowing he'd have almost no groceries at his place, she'd taken over a casserole and some soup. Very casually she had eased into his life, almost as if she belonged there.

Almost—as long as she stayed out of his heart. This particular cowboy was branded tough to tame. But she desperately wanted to tame him.

The question was—could she?

MICHAEL WADE knew himself to be considered a loner, possessed of a personality that earned him few friends but many wary acquaintances. He worked hard. He didn't socialize much; he wasn't interested in clowning around with the single guys in Fallen. Drinking and cutting up weren't his thing, not after he put in long days on the family ranch, which had become his since his dad's death. His mother had moved on a long time before, deciding she could no longer endure her husband suffering with unrequited love for the married Polly Dixon next door. At least that's what one of his high school acquaintances had told him at the time. Michael had taken his mother's desertion personally, though he never let himself think about it anymore. Today wasn't going to be an exception. At thirty, he was a contented bachelor, exactly what a man with common sense ought to be. Women would be a cramp in his life he didn't need.

Not even sweet Bailey Dixon, who got that soft, hopeful gaze in her eyes when he pulled her into bed with him. Maybe he wasn't a gentleman for sleeping with her without intending more than physical pleasure. Maybe he should tell her to put her truck in reverse the next time she came around.

The trouble was, he was selfish. He liked her perky little smile. Her petite, curvy body fit his like his work gloves fit his hands. He enjoyed the way she didn't ask for anything from him. It made it easier to ignore his pangs of conscience, which taunted that perhaps he and his hard-edged father had possessed something in common, after all—their attraction to calm, capable Dixon women.

What further annoyed the hell out of Michael on this crisp February day was that he'd caught himself thinking about Bailey more than once. More than twice. Maybe about twenty times. He found himself glancing toward her ramshackle wooden Victorian house, a half-acre from his, wondering what she was doing. Wondering if she'd come to see him tonight. She did come around, occasionally and uninvited, just when he started missing having someone to talk to and warm him up at the end of a long week.

She hadn't been around in nearly two weeks, and he was about crazy from wondering when she'd be back. He was sorely tempted to ring her number and holler into the phone, "Where the hell are you?"

Something told him that wasn't the appropriate way to draw Bailey to his bed, and he'd never had to invite her before. She just sort of made herself at home.

He blew out a breath in the frigid air, glanced one more time at Bailey's house and turned his horse to head home.

The woman wasn't going to get under his skin.

No way.

"YOU SEE MY PROBLEM," Bailey told her older brother.

"I told you not to mess with him. I told you he wasn't going to marry you," Brad said sourly.

"What you told me doesn't matter now, does it?"

Brad put his head in his hands. "I should go over there and beat his head in. I should shoot him."

"That would upset me greatly." Bailey set milk out for the youngest of the seven Dixon siblings, who were eyeing her and Brad curiously as they spoke in abbreviated terms so the children wouldn't understand the exact content of the conversation. Bailey was twenty-five, and Brad was twenty-six. As for late-in-life accidents, their parents had five of them, now aged five, six, seven, eight and nine. It was like a tap that had been turned on and refused to shut off. Country people who had never strayed from Fallen, they'd married at fifteen, respect for each other forging their family tight-knit and strong. At forty-one, a cruel cancer stole Polly, and not much later, Elijah died of a broken heart, too weak to be willing to go on without his wife.

Contrary to popular belief, it was more than possible to survive on love. It was a richness no coin could purchase.

Their parents had left the family that knowledge, if not money. How to pay the overwhelming inheritance taxes on the house and property fell to Bailey and Brad to figure out. As the eldest, Brad should be head of the household, but he was happier letting Bailey handle most of the practical considerations. Now she'd added a further complication—one more mouth to feed.

She returned to washing dishes. "I knew what I was getting into."

"As the man of this house, it's probably incumbent upon me to at least talk to him."

"No!" Bailey whirled around and eyed her brother sharply. "I'll talk to him. When the time is right."

"The clock is ticking," Brad pointed out. "You need to speed up your timetable."

"Brad," Bailey protested. "Please! It's not going to be easy. I don't know how to tell him...." She fell silent, glancing out the kitchen window to the red-brick, sturdy ranch house Michael's father had commissioned. What little she had of Michael, she didn't want to lose.

Sadness struck her heart. She had a choice to make. She could tell him about the baby, and he'd no doubt do the honorable thing. But she didn't want him that way.

She wanted him to be hers, body and soul and heart and mind.

Not trapped. Not forced—though she knew in her heart it would never happen. He would never feel the way about her she felt about him.

Brad left the kitchen, but Bailey hardly noticed as she stared through the window at the neighboring ranch. "Cowboy, please be mine," she murmured through sudden tears.

"ARE YOU GOING to do any work today?" Chili Haskins turned to look at his loafing companion.

Curly Monroe looked indignant. "Should I?" He settled a bit more comfortably on the wooden fence rail they shared. "We're almost old enough to be members of AARP."

Fred Peters scratched his chin. "You mean that association of retired people? We ain't *that* old."

"Nah." Chili thought that over. "We're fence-sitters, not doing much of anything but sitting on this rail. But we're not retired."

"A fence-sitters' country club," Curly agreed, satisfied. "Kind of exclusive, if you think on it."

"We need to do something, though." Chili wasn't as satisfied as Curly.

"No, we don't. That would defeat the purpose of sitting on the fence," Fred pointed out. "We'd have to turn in our membership in our own club."

"We could do a little more than we're doing to help Michael," Chili argued. "He didn't have to keep us on after his pa passed. He could have sent us packing. I say we help him out some way more than appointing ourselves the unofficial lookouts of the Walking W ranch."

From their vantage point, they gazed at the sprawling ranch house.

"Big place for one person," Fred mentioned.

"Yep. Gotta be lonely." Chili had his two companions in retirement. He wasn't lonely. Michael Wade had no one.

All three men glanced toward the dilapidated Victorian house perched on the opposite hill. Chili cleared his throat. Curly coughed uncomfortably. Fred shifted.

"Been a long time since she's been a-calling," Chili finally said.

"Maybe he ran her off," Curly suggested.

It was a strong possibility. Michael didn't want a whole lot of company, and especially not female, although there wasn't a single unattached woman in all of Fallen who hadn't brought Michael some vittles and a smile. Michael came out every once in a while to jaw with the self-appointed fence-sitters, but as far as they knew, Bailey's nocturnal visits were an amazing exception to his self-imposed seclusion.

"You could casually ask him," Fred said hopefully.

"Ask him if he's seen Bailey lately, as if you didn't know he hasn't."

"He could casually poke me in the honker for butting in!" Chili was indignant. "Any more stupid ideas, *friend?*"

"We could mind our own business," Fred acceded. "That would probably be best."

They were quiet for a while, returning their attention to the ranch house. Michael walked onto the porch, stared at the cloudless sky for a moment, then glanced nonchalantly toward the Victorian before realizing the fence-sitters were watching. He gave a curt wave and retreated into the house.

"If he did run her off, he may be regretting it," Chili noted.

"Sometimes a man doesn't have to say with words what's on his mind," Curly said softly. "I knew he liked that little gal."

Fred sat straighter. "Maybe we could help out."

"How?" Chili demanded. "We're ranch hands, not matchmakers."

"I don't like being retired," Fred stated. "I want to be useful. I want to help Michael, not be a burden."

Curly leaned back on the fence. "If something happened between those two, Bailey is going to be the hard one to convince, I hate to tell ya." It was true. They'd known Bailey since she was a baby. All her twenty-five years she'd been stubborn. If she'd parked her blue truck in her own yard for two weeks, maybe she'd parked it for good where Michael was concerned. It would be tough to convince her to do anything she didn't have a mind to.

They saw the curtain on the west side of the ranch house move slightly before it fell back into place.

Curly's jaw dropped. "He's looking for her!"

"He sure enough is." Fred's tone was filled with astonishment. "Looks like he's got it bad!"

A few moments later, a black truck pulled up the lane to the Victorian house. Bailey, dressed in high heels and a pretty blue dress, hurried from the house and got in before her caller could even ring the doorbell. The truck headed down the lane a second later.

"What is Gunner King fetching Bailey for?" Chili demanded.

"Didn't look like he was fetching her." Fred's voice was even more astonished. "I believe he was calling on her. I never saw him open a car door for anyone else before. And did you get a load of how short Bailey's dress was?"

Curly blinked his eyes rapidly. "I sure as shooting hope the boss didn't see her leave with Gunner."

It might just put the finishing cap on the enmity the two ranchers held. The fence-sitters snapped their gazes to the ranch house just in time to observe Michael heading toward the barn. A few moments later, he tore out on his horse in the opposite direction Bailey had gone.

"I'd say he did see." Chili hopped off the fence, sighing. "Boys, as much as we oughta be enjoying our golden years, we've got work to do. The toughest we ever done."

Curly and Fred slid down to join him.

"They say that force is the only thing that gets two immovable objects together," Chili intoned. "And that two points make a line if you draw it straight enough."

"And that absence makes the heart go wander," Fred added, eager to assist, though misquoting.

"So we got force, two points and a wandering heart," Curly said doubtfully. "What does all that mean?"

Chili picked up his pace. "That if we get caught assisting this situation, Michael may very well kick us off our fence and send us off to the retirement home for doddering ranch help."

"Is there a reason we want to be told to pack our bedrolls?" Curly wondered, hurrying behind him. "I like having the run of his kitchen and den. I like that big-screen TV!"

"Because Michael's father hired us, trained us and kept us when we was just green boys," Chili said over his shoulder. "He kept us on through the lean years when he had to let everybody else go. He treated us like we were something when we couldn't get a job shoveling manure. You think about that, you think about his boy all locked up in his pride. You think about why he is that way, and then you tell me we're not the only ones who can help Michael. And don't expect those young pups he hired to do the job right. Any of the jobs right around here," he said with righteous disgust.

"Isn't that kind of like the blind leading the blind?" Fred asked, puffing to keep up with Chili. "Us helping Michael with his love life?"

"Exactly. And that's the reason we can succeed."

"Because we don't know much about women?" Curly asked.

"All we need to know is that he's happy when Bailey's been by to see him and he's grouchy as all get out now that she ain't." Chili turned to eye them both. "For the sake of old man Wade, we gotta try. Or else Michael's gonna end up like his pa."

"Oh. Bitter and mean," Fred remembered.

"The old folks' home would be better than that," Curly concurred a bit desperately. "You're right. We'll follow your plan."

Chili nodded his appreciation. "Good. Force and two points to tame a wandering heart."

They all knew what lay ahead. It would be more painful than busting a bronc. It would be more back-breaking than branding.

Getting Michael Wade to act on his emotions and tell Bailey how he felt about her would be worse than having wisdom teeth dug out.

It was the ultimate impossible mission. Because where Michael was just a bit unbroken when it came to matters of the heart, Bailey was downright stubborn. More than ornery. Danged one-way, and a female who was as one-way as Bailey wasn't likely to be persuaded to draw the line straight between Michael's point and hers.

Chapter Two

Michael wasn't jealous that Bailey was out with Gunner King. He would never stoop to such an emotion. Clearly, Bailey had thrown him over in favor of his rival, and that was her right. They'd had no commitment, no agreement that they couldn't date whomever they chose.

He leaned back in the saddle and stared into an old pecan tree at an owl, which scrutinized him with unblinking interest. Of course, he would have thought that she wouldn't step out with other men while the two of them were physically involved. That was it. They had shared a physical involvement. Nothing more, but did that mean they could date other people? Not once had the question, nor the desire, entered his mind the entire time Bailey had been coming around. He would have never thought to question whether their situation was monogamous. Plainly, she didn't feel the same way.

If she was trying to make him jealous, it wasn't going to work. His mother had tried to make his father jealous by making goo-goo eyes at Sherman King, Gunner's ever-bachelor divorced father, but she hadn't succeeded. Her husband had possessed an iron grip on his emotions, and so would her son.

He thought about Bailey's mother as he rode slowly toward the house. Polly Dixon had loved her stargazing, painting, ne'er-do-well husband with every ounce of her soul. She would never have played games with his heart. He had been more than man enough where she was concerned. Michael had heard the ranch hands laugh every once in a while as they commented on the sagging porch and the peeling paint of the Dixon home, testament to Mr. Dixon's uselessness. "Whatever ol' Elijah Dixon lacks in muscle, he must make up for in other ways!" They'd laugh. "The ol' guy must have plenty 'tweenst to keep his wife at home with all those young uns!"

Michael tried not to think about the crude remarks. He wouldn't let himself wonder if *he* hadn't possessed enough 'tweenst to satisfy Bailey, making her search for more interesting pastures.

No, he wouldn't allow his mind to travel this torturous path. Life was about iron control.

He rode around the side of the house to the front and glanced toward Bailey's house, the cross-timber rails separating her pie-shaped yard from his less sloped property. She and Gunner had returned, and Gunner was protectively helping Bailey toward her porch, wrapping her coat more closely around her to ward off the chill February wind.

Every ounce of Michael's steely resolve turned into soft, bending ore at the sight of Gunner's arm around his—Michael's—woman. If this was how his father had felt when his mother had flirted with Sherman King, no wonder he'd turned into such a gnarly, difficult old man! "Red-eyed with jealousy, that's what

I am,'' he muttered, as he went to unsaddle his horse. ''So much for iron control.''

There was no controlling Bailey—she was as resilient and headstrong as her mother had been. She'd do whatever she wanted to do, and if she'd thrown him over for Gunner, then there wasn't a whole lot he could do about it except hope his insides didn't feel like worms were tunneling through them forever. He didn't think he could stand it.

When he left the barn, he refused to look at the rambling house again. It hurt too much. Keeping his gaze down as he strode to his porch, he jerked off his leather gloves finger by finger, as if he couldn't remove them without carefully observing his hands.

So he missed the Rodeo Queen standing on his porch, holding a fresh-baked pie that smelled like peach as he hurried to escape inside his house, burning with indignation that Bailey knew he'd seen her date.

''Michael!'' Deenie Day cried with delight. ''I've been wondering where you were!''

''Out riding,'' he replied, not liking her on his porch one bit. He could never think of her as anything except the Rodeo Queen, because she lived her title like some people wore clothes. He'd never seen her without lush, big hair sweeping her skull like a royal mantle and toxifying the air with hair spray fumes. He'd never seen her without her bright, white, toothy smile, as if a camera might pop out from anywhere to take her picture.

''Riding!'' she exclaimed, loud enough for her voice to carry to the neighboring house. ''It's too cold for that, honey! Let's go inside and let me warm you up with some of my *delicious* homemade pie.'' She squeezed his biceps. ''I want to know if it's true that the way to a man's heart is through his tum-tum," she said, patting him there with a hand that lingered.

He was not interested in eating Deenie's peach pie. The Rodeo Queen wanted him to bite into something far more serious than pie, like serious courtship. There was no path to his heart; she and every woman on the planet could save their question for a man interested in answering it.

Five young Dixon children spilled out of the house toward their beloved Bailey, whooping and calling her name as if she'd been gone for a year instead of an hour.

"What a bunch of wild Indians!" Deenie exclaimed. "How can you stand living so near them, hon? All that noise would drive me out of my mind."

He barely heard her, though he thought Deenie could match the children decibel for decibel. He watched Gunner swing the littlest Dixon into his arms and keep the rest from jumping up on Bailey. Smarting with jealousy, he saw Bailey and Gunner suddenly witness Deenie's presence with interest, and though his mind warned him he really didn't want to do this, he allowed her to pull him inside his house with a well-manicured hand.

"Now, then," she said silkily, "you just sit right down and I'll warm this up in the microwave so it's good and *hot*."

Michael stared into Deenie's determined eyes and knew he was in big trouble. She had far more on her mind than getting the pie good and hot, and red-eyed idiot that he was, he had let her inside his house, his only refuge.

He wished uncomfortably that Bailey would make one of her appearances before matters got too far out of hand, before Deenie got to where she was really heated up, but as he glanced out the kitchen window while Deenie's back was turned, he saw Gunner and Bailey go inside her house.

Michael was on his own.

BAILEY COULDN'T BELIEVE she'd gotten sick to her stomach in front of Gunner. It was so humiliating! She had hoped that her nausea would hold off for the time it would take her to discuss the employment opportunity Gunner was offering. Secretarial duties at his home office four hours a day during the week would bring her a badly needed income, and most importantly, keep her near the children. Though Brad was a wonderful caregiver and loved watching their siblings—he liked to sketch and paint them—five rowdy bodies under the age of ten was a lot for anyone to handle. They had agreed she should listen to Gunner's offer. She'd gone with him to see his office setup and learn everything her job would entail.

And had been horribly ill not ten minutes after she'd walked into the enormous King mansion. The cook had been preparing sausage links and beef tacos for the hands, and though she'd tried to fight off the green sensation stealing through her insides, she had barely made it to the bathroom Gunner swiftly helped her to.

Gunner had brought her home and assisted her to the worn red-and-white check sofa to sit. Her mother had loved to sit here and gaze out the big window at her children playing while she folded laundry. Bailey felt a twinge sitting in her mother's place, almost as if she could feel her mother's presence.

I've let Mother down, Bailey thought sadly.

Gunner stood, staring at her with concerned eyes

she could hardly meet. She had to tell him something. This was the most ill she'd been during her pregnancy. For a shaky moment, she thought about writing the condom company and telling them they had boasted about their product a bit too proudly, but mostly she wanted the awful moment to pass. She thought about telling Gunner she must have eaten food that didn't agree with her or that she had a bad flu, but he'd soon enough begin wondering why a watermelon was growing under her coat. It couldn't be much longer before she started to show. Gunner looked so worried she didn't have the heart to fib for the sake of her pride.

"Gunner, I'm really not the candidate you need for your office job," she said miserably, "as much as I would like to take you up on your offer. You're very kind to try to help us out." Gunner and everybody else knew that the Dixons were having huge trouble meeting the large inheritance tax owed on the property. "It's just that I'm…expecting." She couldn't meet his eyes as she said the words.

Brad shooed the children from the room. Bailey heard them go upstairs as Gunner knelt in front of her. He swept a lock of hair from her face and dabbed at moisture on her upper lip. "Let's talk about this later. You need to be in bed."

She heard the kindness in his voice and wished desperately it was Michael offering her the same caring. "I think I'm fine. It seems to come and go like that, suddenly."

He got up and sat beside her. "Bailey, you're in a real pickle here. You've got to let me help you out. You can't go on taking care of this house and these kids and yourself and be beating yourself up about the IRS, too."

Embarrassment burned through her. She couldn't speak.

"It's Michael's, isn't it?"

She forced herself to meet his gaze. "How do you know?"

"By the look on his face tonight when he saw me with you. If looks could kill, I'd be hanging up for the vultures right now." He laughed. "I kind of enjoyed getting his goat for a minute."

"You guys have been at each other for years. My daddy used to say that if our house hadn't been sitting right smack in the middle to keep your families apart, you would have been Fallen's own Hatfields and McCoys."

Gunner laughed again. "Nah. That was between his dad and mine. I got sent to the University of Texas, Michael got sent to A&M just so the rivalry could pick up another chapter, I believe. But I never paid any attention to it, and I hoped Michael didn't. Except now that he's seen me with you, no doubt a new chapter's going to be written."

"You don't sound sorry about it." Bailey tried to sound stern, but Gunner's grin was too big not to return.

"I figure if Michael wants to sit in his house like a big damn bear with a chip on his shoulder, that's his problem. He doesn't know, does he?"

"No." Bailey lowered her eyelashes. "I don't know how to tell him."

"Well," Gunner said, getting to his feet, "I don't know what you see in him, Bailey Dixon. I've never understood what any of the women saw in him. They must go for those strong, silent types." He settled his hat onto his head. "You go rest. My offer still stands. In fact, I'll make you another one."

"You've already been more than generous, Gunner," she said softly.

"If you can't get that lunkhead across the way to marry you and give your baby a name, I'll be more than happy to do it. You just say the word."

Her lips parted as she stared into his brown eyes. "Gunner King! What are you saying?"

"What I shoulda said a long time ago. What I was trying to get to before your ma took ill." The smile was gone from his face, the light dimming in his eyes. "I had just about worked up the courage to ask you out when I found out about your mother, Bailey. I thought it was best to wait. I knew you had all you could handle at the time. Now I see I should have spoken up sooner, but I've had my eyes on you, Bailey Dixon. I have for a long time."

Bailey gasped. "Are you telling me this because you think Michael was upset that you were with me tonight? If this is some more rivalry stuff, I can tell you right now I'm not going to be caught in the middle!"

"No." He took her chin between his fingers, shaking his head. "I told you, I don't care about my father's and Michael's father's antagonizing. I can't stand to see you worrying when I could make your life so much easier."

"I don't love you, Gunner," she said unhappily.

"I know that." His lips thinned. "The girls always go for him. Women seem to like a man who presents a challenge. I'd not be much of a challenge for you, Bailey. And I would treat you like the ground you walked on was sacred."

Her breath caught. She moved away from the fingers that held her chin so gently. "Gunner, I don't know what to say."

He nodded. "I figured as much. I'll give you time to work out your situation with Michael. I gotta tell you, I don't think he's going to marry you."

"I know." She could feel the pink of mortification rising in her cheeks.

"Well, I've made my best offer." He slapped his gloves against his jeans and pulled them on. "It'd be better for your baby to be with its real father, I know that. And I'd honestly like for you to take on my employment offer, because the truth is there aren't a whole lot of people I'd trust with knowing the specifics of my finances. If it comes to be that you can't get that stubborn old goat to go the way you need him, you let me know. Until then, our relationship remains strictly business."

"Thanks, Gunner." Bailey could feel her hands trembling from her astonishment. Never had she imagined Gunner felt this way! "I really appreciate that."

"All right, then. If you want the job, start Monday. I'll leave instructions as to what I need organized and what billings I want you to set up on a payment schedule. Your assistance will be greatly appreciated, I can assure you."

She stared at him, waiting for him to finish.

"I'll be out on the ranch, Bailey, while you're working. I rarely have reason to come back to the house before lunch." He tipped his hat to her. "Be seeing you."

"Goodbye," she murmured through stiff lips. She saw him to the door, managing a frozen smile as she closed the door behind him.

Then she put her head in her hands and told herself she wouldn't cry. She wouldn't. Not over Michael Wade.

The doorbell rang. Bailey stiffened, wondering if Gunner might have quickly decided to snatch back one or both of his offers. She pulled the door open again, looking out cautiously.

Chili Haskins stood on her porch, his white, bushy mustache like icicles above his lips. "Howdy, Bailey."

"Hello, Chili." She glanced behind him, but Michael was nowhere to be seen. "What can I do for you?"

"We—uh, I was wondering if you could come over to the Walking W for a minute. Fred Peters has got hisself in an embarrassing predicament, and the boss is, uh, busy, so we wondered, I mean, we hoped, well, with all these tykes running around, we figured you're the one who has the savvy to help us out."

She blinked, uncertain as to whether she wanted to step foot on the Walking W if the boss was busy with Deenie Day.

"Please, Miz Bailey," Chili prompted, "we sure could use your assistance, sooner than later!"

Chapter Three

The only way Deenie managed to get a forkful of pie into Michael's mouth was that his jaw dropped when Bailey swished through the kitchen door behind Chili. "Bailey!" He jumped to his feet, chewing as fast as he could and swallowing guiltily. Deenie stood ready to land another forkful between his lips if he wasn't careful. "What are you doing here?"

"Hello, Deenie." Laser-blue eyes turned on Michael with cool acknowledgment. "Chili asked me to come over and take a look at Fred Peters. We didn't mean to interrupt your…dessert." She swept the laden fork Deenie held with a meaningful glance.

Michael wiped his mouth with a napkin as he took in Bailey's blue dress, which was far too short and feminine to warrant wearing in this cold weather—and certainly too short to be worn in the vicinity of Gunner King. His heart froze as he imagined Gunner touching Bailey's silky-smooth legs. "We were finished," he said abruptly. "Why didn't you come get me, Chili?"

"Because we knew you were busy," Chili replied accusingly. "We didn't want to interrupt."

He saw the pink spots burning in Bailey's cheeks

but put it down to wind chap. "There's nothing to interrupt. Where's Fred?"

"In the TV room." Chili hurried out, and after one last glance at the pie and Deenie, Bailey followed him without so much as another look at Michael. He'd been hoping the woman would come around for the better part of two weeks, and when she finally did, she acted like he was no more than a neighbor. He wondered how close Gunner was managing to get to his girl and decided it was better not to speculate.

"Excuse me," Michael said to Deenie, hurrying after Chili. He heard her boots behind his and wished she'd taken the hint to stay put.

To his amazement, Fred lay flat on his back on the carpet, his sock-clad foot caught in an automatic putting cup.

"What in blazes are you doing, Fred?" Michael demanded.

Bailey had knelt beside the skinny cowboy and was examining where his toes disappeared inside the mechanical device. "You're stuck good," she told him. "Does it hurt?"

"Not much." Fred grunted the words, but it was clear he was humiliated and in pain. "I shouldn't have kicked the stupid golf ball into the cup. But I lost my temper. I just can't putt like Nicklaus."

"Oh, for crying out loud." Michael couldn't believe what he was hearing—or seeing. "Since when did you take up golf?"

"Since we thought about retiring," Fred said woefully. "We heard it was what a fellow did with his free time."

Bailey lifted Fred's foot gently, holding the cup so it wouldn't pull on his toes. "Let's see if we can force some of the blood back into your foot so the swelling might go down and loosen you up.''

"I have never seen anything so ridiculous in my whole life," Deenie stated.

The three cowboys favored her with a baleful stare. She plopped into a chair and stared at the TV screen, where it was Greg Norman's turn to putt. "Now, there's a man who probably knows what to do with his putter," she said to the room at large.

Bailey turned and gave Deenie her most disgusted frown. "Deenie, could you please make yourself useful and bring me some ice? Since you're acquainted with the kitchen?"

This she directed his way, Michael noticed with displeasure. "I'll get it," he said quickly, not wanting Bailey to think he was helpless the way her father had been. "You stay right there," he said to Deenie.

"I'll wait for you, Michael," she murmured with a sweet smile for Bailey's sake.

He couldn't be bothered with that silly remark. Fred was clearly in pain, so he hurried off to do Bailey's bidding. When he returned, she had the putter unplugged, Fred's foot elevated against an ottoman, and she was peering up his ankle into the cup.

"Maybe I should take a look," Michael offered.

"No!" Fred cried. "Don't let him, Bailey! He'll leave my toes in there!"

"Michael!" Bailey's glance was stern. "I can handle this! You're just making matters worse, upsetting poor Fred."

"I—" He held out the ice in a plastic container. He'd been trying to assist her, and already she thought he was a lost cause. Poor Fred, indeed. He was milking

Bailey's warmth and sunshine like a professional con man.

"What a crybaby!" Deenie leaned back in the chair and curled her legs underneath her. "I've fallen off horses and not cried as loud as you are."

"Maybe it's because once you had that lobotomy, you lost all feeling," someone muttered under his or her breath.

"Who said that?" Michael demanded. He couldn't tell, but he didn't think it had been Bailey. Her eyes were amazingly serene and innocent. "There's no reason for rudeness."

Bailey sighed. "Michael, maybe you could take Deenie to the kitchen and get her a glass of tea. I think Fred could relax more if his every move wasn't being scrutinized. I'll have him out of this raccoon trap in a jiff."

She really did think he was helpless. And in his own house! "All right," Michael said, defeated. "Deenie, let's head back to the kitchen."

"Gladly." She shot Bailey a pleased smile as she exited the room.

Bailey patted Fred's cheek when they were gone. "You nearly got yourself in big trouble."

"I know." His lips were pinched with pain. "I'm not the kindest person when I don't feel good. I broke my arm once when the old man was alive, and as he was taking me to the hospital, I told him what a sorry-ass, son of—"

"I get your drift." Bailey smiled at him. "I'm not myself when I don't feel good, either. Most people aren't."

"Is he going to have to go to the hospital?" Curly asked worriedly. "He doesn't like it much when he goes. Doesn't care for women in white—nurses or brides.''

"No.'' Gingerly, she put her fingers into the cup and felt where Fred's toes were obstructed.

"We tried poking tongs in there, but he hollered something fierce and my fingers are too durn big,'' Chili said sorrowfully. "We knew you could probably do the trick.''

"And this once, I can.'' Gently, she released Fred's toes and slid the device off, revealing red and angry marks on his skin. "You'd better keep your foot up for a while.''

He scooched to a chair and heaved himself in it. Curly propped a pillow underneath his friend's foot. "Shoo! I thought I was going to lose a toe! Bless you, Miss Bailey.''

"You're welcome, Fred.'' She got to her feet. "I'd better get home. If you don't mind, Chili, I think I'll go out the front door instead of the kitchen door.''

"I'd rather myself,'' he agreed. "She's an alligator!''

Bailey laughed but hurt all the more for knowing that Michael must like the Rodeo Queen if he was eating her pie, from her fork, no less. "You fellows be careful. Good night.''

"Good night!'' Curly and Fred called.

Chili opened the front door, motioning her through before he closed it behind them.

"You don't have to walk me home, Chili.''

"I'd never let a lady make her way in the dark alone.''

"All right.'' She tried not to think of all the times she'd slid out of Michael's bed before dawn—before the children awakened and looked for her, before anyone might see her truck and before he'd need to get up to tend his chores. Michael had never once offered to even walk her down the stairs. "Chili, do you think he likes her?" she asked, unable to help herself.

"Nope. I think he likes you," he said eagerly, obviously comfortable in a Dear Abby role, "if he could just figure out how to tell ya, I just know he would."

"Why do you think so?" Bailey's heart beat faster with hope.

"I dunno. Just a funny feeling I had that Michael thought pretty much of you."

"He didn't like Fred's lobotomy remark." Michael had taken up for Deenie *fast*.

"Yeah, but he doesn't like rudeness for much of any reason. Michael believes his every emotion should be kept under lock and key. 'Course, most folks can't live that way."

She sure couldn't! She felt like she might blow up from the thought of Deenie putting her lips where she'd put her fork—Michael's mouth. But he was right. Just because Deenie was being a pain didn't mean anyone else should follow her lead. She wished she were better at being like Michael. Maybe she wouldn't be hurting so much right now. Fred had only given voice to the very thoughts Bailey had been guilty of thinking about Deenie.

So she took Chili's assurance that Michael liked her as comfort, even though she didn't believe it wholeheartedly. Michael had never had *her* over in the light of day.

"The question is, do you like him?"

She felt the cowboy's cagey gaze on her face. If she wasn't careful, she might reveal more than she should—and she didn't want her secret sprung on Michael until she had a chance to tell him herself. "I...I don't know. I'm not sure he's looking for anyone to like him," she replied carefully.

"He's not good at romance, Bailey. Women are not Michael's specialty."

"You could have fooled me!" Bailey shot back.

"Oh, don't let Deenie stir your pot. She's a man-trap. Mind you, he's going to be long in figuring out how to tell you how he feels, if he ever does," Chili stated. "You'll have to be mighty patient, more patient than a saint, Bailey. Michael won't let his feelings just spew out of him like a valve letting off. But given enough time, you just might win the day. That is, if *you* want *him*."

Oh, I do. Bailey closed her eyes. She'd been patient for six months, all her life, really, hoping Michael would learn to love her. Say the words she wanted to hear.

She'd simply run out of time.

DEENIE AND MICHAEL watched Chili help Bailey over the wooden cross-timber fence that separated the two properties. Bailey barely made it over before the youngest Dixons met her, jumping around her like anxious puppies. The cries of greeting to their big sister could be heard by anyone within a ten-mile radius.

"That place is the Indigent Ranch," Deenie said scornfully. "The county ought to condemn that house. Why don't the Dixons move if they can't take care of the place? I don't believe they've ever fixed a shingle on the dump the hundred years it's been barely standing. Really, Michael, it's such an eyesore next to your lovely home."

She glanced at her rhinestone-covered blue jean

jacket, which sparkled and flashed in the light, like her teeth and blond hair. Deenie was all-over perfection, a showgirl.

Michael wistfully thought about Bailey's warmth and caring. If the two women's lives were reversed, Bailey would be thinking about how she could do something to help Deenie, not put her down because of her lack of money. But Deenie had always been attracted to that which counted on the surface, which looked great on the outside. He supposed most folks were. Which made Bailey all the more special. He admired her for taking on the responsibilities of a brother who wasn't cut out for being head of a family and for shouldering the burden of overseeing such a large household. It had to be harder than anything he was doing, Michael thought with some discomfort.

"Go easy on Bailey, Deenie. She's had it rough since her mom and dad died."

"She's had it rough all her life." Deenie shook her head. "I feel sorry for her. But you've got to admit, Michael, Bailey brings a lot of her misery on herself."

He frowned. "How's that?"

"Well, she'd have a man by now if she'd do something with herself!" Deenie exclaimed. "Then she wouldn't be living hand to mouth like side-of-the-road trash, would she?"

"I don't think Bailey's the type of woman who would look around for a man to solve her problems."

"I didn't say that, Michael, I said she'd have one by now and all her problems would be solved!" Deenie looked at him like he was nuts. "Bailey's too stubborn to try, though. I told her in high school if she'd put that straggly blond hair up on her head, or even cut a few inches off of it, it would look so much nicer around her face. Give her a little glamour. Do you know what she told me?''

Michael couldn't wait to hear. ''What?''

''That she liked her hair just fine!'' Deenie was outraged. ''Have you ever heard the like? Who wants hair hanging down to their waist and flat as a price tag at Neiman Marcus? It's all fine for high school, but she's got to be nearly twenty-six now, and she still won't do anything with herself.''

Michael suppressed the smile that leaped to his lips. Deenie probably spent more in a month on hair spray and lipstick than Bailey spent all year on food. Truth was, he liked Bailey's clean skin and long, soft hair. It teased the top of her fanny when she was naked, it framed her face when she was asleep, far more glamorous than Deenie's hard-packed big hair, which probably wouldn't even move on a pillow. As for glamour, well, Bailey looked like she belonged in a Victoria's Secret photo shoot, as far as he was concerned.

''Now the length of her dress was better tonight, short and fashionable,'' Deenie continued, ''but the only reason it was so short was because it was shrunk. It's been washed a thousand times. That was the same navy dress her mother used to wear to pick the kids up from school. Only now it's powder blue from fading.''

''Deenie,'' Michael said abruptly, ''you ought to set your sights on Gunner King.''

''Gunner!'' Deenie stared at him. ''Why, hon?'' She ran her gaze over his shoulders hungrily. ''He's not nearly as sexy as you are.''

''Got a lot more money,'' Michael stated ever so casually. He didn't know if that was true, but a glance outside the window revealed Chili on his way over the fence. If he could send Deenie packing, he might have time to pick the cowboys' brains about Bailey.

"More money?" Deenie echoed. "How do you know?"

"Oh, his father made a killing in some oil well down south before he died." Michael shrugged. "Heard they made so much money on it that they were thinking about buying a winter home in Rio." He paused as Deenie's eyes dilated. "Of course, that wouldn't do Gunner any good now. No fun to vacation alone."

"Rio!" Deenie exclaimed. "Oh, my goodness, would you look at the time? I'd better be going." She snatched up her pie, examining it carefully. "It doesn't look like somebody took a bite out of it," she said under her breath. "It just looks like the crust caved in a little." Turning toward the door, she gave Michael her best Rodeo Queen smile. "Call me sometime, sugar."

She was gone in a flash of expensive perfume. Michael shuddered. It was almost cruel to sic Deenie on his rival, but Gunner no doubt would somehow return the favor one day.

"Two of a kind," he muttered. Striding down the long hall toward the enormous TV room, he saw Chili and Curly helping Fred to his feet.

"I'll drive him home," Michael said. "He doesn't need to be walking down to the bungalow."

"Thanks, Michael." Chili glanced at him. "Where's the wasp?"

"What wasp?"

"The skinny, stinging female with her feelers out." Chili shot him a disgruntled look.

"Oh, Deenie. Gone off to build her nest somewhere

else, I hope." Michael moved the two cowboys aside and put his arm under Fred's for support. "Slow and careful, Fred."

He fit his pace to the older man's. "Are you sure you don't want me to run you down to the quack shack? Maybe you ought to have a doc look at it."

There was some swelling of Fred's toes, but the cowboy gamely shook his head. "Nope. Bailey didn't mention I oughta go, so I'm sure it's fine."

"Maybe Bailey isn't a doctor."

"Maybe Bailey's just as good as that quack in town," Fred shot back. "She's been coping with kiddie emergencies since she was old enough to help Polly out."

It was a bit of a raw spot with Michael. When his mother left, the cowboys began slinking over to Polly's whenever they had something that needed more tending than they could handle. Polly Dixon had a never-ending supply of ointment, bandages, good humor and compassion. "Doc Watson's a fine doctor. And Deenie was right. You're crybabies," he said, helping Fred into the truck bed. "You just want your ouchies kissed."

"Damn right," Fred shot back, "and if you was smart, son, you'd let Bailey kiss *yours*."

The cowboys murmured their agreement. Michael hesitated. Then he decided he didn't want to know whatever was going around in their white-thatched heads. "You fellows don't have enough to do," he said crustily. "Tomorrow I want you to check every inch of the fence and make sure it's secure." He gave them all a baleful glare. "Particularly the area around the Dixon pond. I don't want any of my cattle getting mixed in with Gunner's or getting spooked by the Dixon sheep.''

The large pond was the only valuable thing the Dixons owned. It lay in a liquid, undulating circle at the top of their property. It was the only nearby water source, and both Sherman King and Michael Wade Senior had eyed it for their cattle. Because Elijah said he couldn't trust either of the feuding ranchers to behave like gentlemen, he'd allowed them both the use of it, but insisted that they each run a separate fence divider through the portion he allotted them. Therefore the pond was evenly split three ways. He charged the ranchers a yearly fee for the use, a pittance compared to what they'd pay to have city water pumped in. Elijah had said it was worth using the clear, clean water to cool off the hotheads living on either side of him.

Then old Elijah had got him a few sheep, which stared at the big-horned beasts on either side of them but otherwise paid no attention. The hands said Elijah was so bone-idle he kept the sheep so he wouldn't have to mow his yard. Indeed, the sheep did keep the grass short clear up to the porch. Michael suspected the old man had been less lazy than a peacekeeping dreamer. Sheep were quiet and gentle, and the Dixon children played with them as if they were dogs. Everybody was happy.

Except his employees right now. They stared at him accusingly.

"Every inch," he reiterated. "I don't need any more reasons for you to be running to the Dixon house."

They were silent.

"Of course, if you like it over there so much, if you've become so shiftless that you need a woman constantly fussing over you, I'm sure she'd be more than happy to take you in.'' He knew he was being cruel, but the comment about letting Bailey kiss his hurts had stung—worse than Deenie's waspiness.

"Hardheaded sourpuss like his old man,'' one of them whispered.

"No, I'm not.'' Michael straightened indignantly.

"You are! And the minute that rhinestone cowgirl gets her hooks in ya, she's going to put us out!'' Fred cried.

"Neither Deenie nor Bailey is going to become part of the Wade household,'' Michael stated with a firm edge to his tone. "If that's what's got you all riled up, let me be the first to assure you that you are going nowhere, and I am not headed to the altar.''

They frowned but said no more. Michael nodded and moved to get into the truck cab.

"Michael,'' Chili called.

He paused. "Yes?''

"Did you know Gunner's offered Bailey a secretarial position at his place?''

Michael's mouth instantly dried out. Her short, faded skirt appeared in his mind, and all that smooth skin, which shouldn't have been exposed to such cold weather.

Gunner's stately home would be very warm inside.

The cowboys stared at him, their eyes bugging and curious in the darkness as they sat in the truck bed. He forced himself to shrug.

"Everybody's gotta do what they gotta do,'' he said noncomittally.

But his heart was hammering inside him like a town pep rally parade drum. Not a date, then! Gunner was too smart for that—Bailey had rarely dated anyone.

Employing Bailey was even more insidious than just asking her out, which she most likely would have refused. She needed money, and Gunner had given her a way to get it without costing her pride.

It was very slick.

If his rival had his eyes on a new acquisition, Michael's territory would be encroached.

There was no fence he could secure to protect what he considered he should have some kind of claim on.

I am not jealous, he reminded himself. *Bailey's always done what she wanted to do, and nothing's going to change that now.*

He blew out a breath, glared at the cowboys, stiffened his shoulders and got in the truck cab. Gunner King had always been a burr in his sock, only he couldn't pick him out and throw him away like a burr. Looked like he planned on sticking to Bailey like a burr.

Michael's blood pressure soared. There was no hope for it. He was going to have to do something.

He had to match his rival for slickness and stickiness.

Maybe the cowboys were right. After all, they were a study in slick and burr sticky! If he needed a crash course in charm to keep Gunner from stealing his woman, then Michael had three good-luck charms riding in his truck bed right now. Maybe all it took was playing on Bailey's sympathetic, warm nature to lure her to his side.

He opened the small window that separated the cab from the truck bed. "Hey."

"What?" They craned their necks to see him.

"I don't think Bailey working in Gunner's home would be the best thing for her."

"Eh?" Chili cocked his head.

"I was thinking maybe there was a better way she could spend her time." He eyed them, taking note of their interest. "After all her family's done for you, I know you wouldn't want Bailey's situation taken advantage of by the Kings or anyone else. Maybe ya'll could come up with something and sort of suggest it to me."

The three studies in slick and sticky grinned. "You just let us be your suggestion box, boss," Chili informed him. "But you gotta promise to go along with our ideas. If you butt heads with us at every turn…well, Gunner's gonna make his move."

Michael hesitated, wondering just what he was getting himself into.

"Ya snooze, ya lose, boss," Fred told him.

"He's got a point," Curly chimed in, "you gotta admit you're kinda short on sensitivity to the garden-variety female."

"You ain't had much practice," Fred said more forthrightly. "You're kinda like a grumpy ol' mule. Got the stuff, but ain't quite sure what to do with it."

"All right, all right," Michael interrupted swiftly so he wouldn't have to hear any more about his failings. There was only so much a man could take before he lost his nerve! Bailey was no garden-variety female— she was a wildflower that would require significant patience and wooing unless he wanted her growing in Gunner's garden two fences away from him. "No guts, no glory. The suggestion box is open."

They waited expectantly.

"And not resistant to your ideas," he said, relenting.

Chili grinned. "You just leave everything to us."

Michael nodded and closed the window. "I'm just doing her the same favor I'd do for anyone the King machinery was about to flatten," he muttered as he started the ignition. "*Somebody's* got to save that headstrong little woman from herself!"

Chapter Four

"Now, then," Chili said, giving Michael's dark suit a final brush across the shoulders, "you just drive over to the Dixon house and surprise that little gal by picking her and her brood up for church." The fence-sitters had converged on him with Plan A as he was eating breakfast, before he'd even had time to gulp enough coffee to wake up good.

Michael shook his head. "I don't know that this is such a good idea. Bailey and I have never gone anywhere together, much less *church*." Something about these three advising him to go to church with a woman struck his suspicion nerve very hard. He never went to church. Whatever he had to say to the Lord he said on his property amongst the trees and the stillness. Saying it in front of a bunch of people didn't mean the Lord's ears were open any further to him.

But the townsfolks' ears and eyes would be wide open if he appeared with Bailey Dixon. There were two types of couples who paired up for church—good friends comfortable celebrating the Sabbath with each other, often seen in Fallen's Baptist church with its social congregation, and those affianced or about to be who attended church to start their marriage out on the right foot. He'd noted the Fallen Methodists tended to do a lot of that.

He was neither Baptist nor Methodist, nor much of anything that required a commitment. And he wasn't friends with Bailey, nor trying to start a relationship with her aligned on the straight and narrow path. It was too late for that, he supposed.

He'd have to go to the Catholic church with Bailey, and that was enough to make him nervous. Bailey *and* her six siblings—thankfully she had felt condoms were necessary for the relationship they'd shared. The Rodeo Queen had been right about one thing—the Dixon family was like a very full cup, which runneth over and spilled down the table leg and flooded a good-size room. He wondered if there was a sermon in that.

He just hoped five-year-old Baby didn't bring her lamb to church. Surely Bailey made her leave her pet at home. Sheep turds in the nice Lincoln town car his father had owned were likely to turn his stomach this early in the morning.

"Michael, I know you're not eager about this," Fred said, carefully standing off the toes that still pained him from last night's putting debacle. "This is the only day you have before Bailey starts work for Gunner, so it's an opportune time to make your move and make yourself look good. Bailey's going to drag those young 'uns to church, and you just think about them shivering in that rattletrap metal truck bed she totes that family around in when they could be warm in your car with its heater and cushioned seats. The inch of snow we had last night isn't going to stop Bailey from seeing those kids get proper churchin'."

Michael sighed, and it was an unwilling sound of

resignation. "Couldn't I just drop them off and pick them up?"

"No!" Curly stated emphatically. "You know, Michael, it's not going to kill you to spend an hour with the top of your head being reviewed by the Lord."

"Why aren't you going, then?" Michael demanded.

"We ain't in the trouble with Bailey that you are." Chili crossed his arms. "You're the one who wants to save her from herself. Taking her to church is the best way I can think of to start the process—and you get the jump on Gunner. She may start work for him tomorrow, but she'll have been to church with you today."

It might not be the proper thought, but he'd much rather Bailey be in bed with him *tonight*. Still, he couldn't say that to the cowboys—they were in their fatherly capacity, which they'd adopted as of last night's agreement to save Bailey.

"Guess I wouldn't want those kids to freeze to death." He jammed on a black felt hat, which matched his formal suit, clothes he hadn't worn since his father's funeral. He felt stiff and out of place in these duds, and the sensation was sure to increase in the next few moments.

He warmed up the car, then backed down the driveway and headed to Bailey's. Leaving the roomy car running, he strode up the bent-in-the-middle porch and stabbed the doorbell impatiently.

Baby opened the door, her little lamb at her side. Michael held back an inward groan. "Where's Bailey, Baby?"

"Upstairs." Baby put her finger in her mouth, which Michael thought couldn't be all that sanitary considering the beast beside her. But she was dressed for church, just as the cowboys had predicted.

Brad appeared in a suit that was frayed at the cuffs and shoes that were wafer-thin in the sole. Michael felt slightly ashamed of his dude's suit he'd just been thinking ill thoughts over. It was nicer than anything anyone in this house owned, and it didn't matter that he felt like the Grim Reaper in it. He should be more appreciative of what he was able to buy. This family was up to their eyeballs in trying to pay off the tax man.

"Come in, Michael. How can we help you?" Brad asked.

That gave Michael a start. *How can they help me*— and then he realized that it was always his family or the cowboys who went to the Dixon house for one thing or another. Not once had they come to the wealthy Wade holding for assistance of any kind. The thought was humbling, and slightly embarrassing. "I thought to offer your family a ride to church," he said gruffly.

"You don't go to our church." Brad looked at Michael curiously.

"Won't hurt me to go once to any church." Michael instinctively stiffened as four more children grouped around him, all dressed in hand-me-down clothing. "Got the car warming. What do you say?"

"It's up to Bailey." Brad shifted the burden of decision-making to his sister, jerking his head toward the stairs. "I'll ask her."

Bailey appeared at the top of the stairs at that moment. "Michael? I thought I heard your voice."

She walked down, and he felt more nervous than he had at his first high school dance. She was plainly startled to see him, and her blond brows arched over large blue eyes. The tiny freckles he thought so sassy lightly sprinkled her nose. And that glorious hair he loved fell shiny and bright as new gold to her waist, without a hint of curl in it.

She was so sexy she made his knees feel like they might start knocking together. He tried to smile, but his hands were trembling and he was afraid she'd notice, so the smile slipped away. Having never asked Bailey to go anywhere with him, this was one tough assignment the cowboys had sent him on.

"Thought I'd take your crew to church. It's mighty cold outside."

"You needn't have worried about us." She looked at him steadily, a light scent of soap carrying from her skin. "We'll manage."

So true to this stubborn woman's nature not to accept anything from anyone. How had Gunner managed with such ease? *By not stepping on her pride.* He cleared his throat. "It's been a while since I've been to church," he said softly, his eyes on hers. "Wouldn't mind sitting with friends."

She smiled, happiness crinkling the corners of her eyes and lifting the sides of her beautiful lips. "Well, if you can handle sitting in church with my crowd, then we'll be happy to accept your offer."

He nodded, but his insides were singing with joy. Gunner didn't have anything on *him* for slick and burr sticky! He'd get it all figured out soon enough; practice made perfect, and he might even start to enjoy his new role as Bailey's protector.

BAILEY HAD TO FIGHT giggles all through the hour-long service. Michael had no idea what he'd gotten

himself into with his generous offer! She hoped he had
a patron saint keeping watch on him, because during
the last fifty-five minutes, his lap had been a continual
seat for one Dixon child or the other. The nine-year-
old, Beth, was too big to sit in his lap so she settled
for sitting beside him, proudly helping him find where
he should be reading in the church booklet or the hym-
nal. Brad stared straight ahead, but Bailey had seen
the sides of his mouth twitching. The big cowboy from
the Wade ranch could handle steers, but he had his
hands full with little people.

Bailey closed her eyes, the smile erased from her
lips. He'd really be bowled over if he knew a tiny
person was on the way, one that would bear his fea-
tures in some fashion. Her insides went cold. She
couldn't refuse his request to sit with friends, as he'd
put it, knowing how uncomfortable he'd be in a church
by himself. His father had been more likely to have a
pact with the devil than peace with the Lord, and that
was true even before his wife left him. Before they
separated, the Wades didn't attend church with their
only child. Mrs. Wade had once confided to a town
gossip that she didn't reckon she could sit beside her
husband for an hour anywhere without getting into an
argument.

Bailey pressed her lips together. No, she would
never have turned Michael away, knowing how miserable he'd be forcing himself to walk inside a church
alone and sit there for an hour the subject of scrutiny.
Afterward, single women would take advantage of the
opportunity to flirt with him and cozy up to the Wade
fortune. Like a deer tentatively making its way from
the cover of woods, he'd be a prime target in the clearing for manhunters.

But she was going to have to figure out a way eventually to inform him that they were far more than friends.

They were soon-to-be parents.

WHEN THE HOUR was over, Michael breathed a huge sigh of victory. He'd made it! Only one crayon had rolled under the pew—rescued—one child's shoe clattered loudly to the floor—rescued—and one bulletin had fluttered from a child's hand to the floor in front of the altar. Rescued, by the kindly priest, who smiled at him and the passel of kids who insisted on sitting in his lap. Why did the Dixons have to sit in the front row, in front of the entire congregation and the choir and the religious personnel? Though they didn't make a peep, the children were like a shifting landscape, never still except during the sermon.

That still had him amazed.

And only one bathroom break had been required—Bailey's, to his astonishment. She hadn't looked well when she hurried suddenly to the back of the church. Her skin had taken on a pasty look, pronounced by the bright sunlight streaming through the stained glass. Maybe she wasn't getting good food to eat.

He could fix that.

Outside the church, as they all crammed into his Lincoln—had he ever thought this car was roomy?—he said, "Let me take everyone to the pancake house as my way of thanks."

He slid his gaze to Bailey, who stared over Baby, planted firmly between them. Brad sat in the back, the extra children packed on and around him and breaking the law for seat-belt safety, no doubt. Some kids were double-belted, some perched on his lap, but Brad seemed oblivious to the crowding.

Michael admired his patience. Bailey was shaking her head to his offer, and he was afraid he'd lose his.

"You need not treat us for such a simple thing as going to church together. We've already had the enjoyment of your car, and that's enough," she said firmly.

But he'd heard the gasps from the back seat. The children likely hadn't been out to eat in their entire lives. A pancake house was temptation beyond belief. "Please, Bailey," he murmured, "let me do something small for the children."

"It's not small!" she replied under her breath. "Feeding all of us will cost a fortune, and we don't have any way of splitting the tab with you."

He saw the steel in her posture. But he was determined to have his way on this, now that he'd heard the delight from the too-well-mannered children who wouldn't dare erupt in pleas, but who were no doubt hoping he'd somehow change Bailey's mind.

"Bailey." He made his voice low and pleading.

"You wouldn't enjoy a meal with this bunch." She turned her head and looked out the window. "Thank you, but no."

Her stiff spine said clearly, *We're not a charity case.*

Surely she knew he didn't feel that way. There had to be something else making her dig in and refuse to share a few five-pancake stacks at Miss Nary's Pancakes and Dairy. "I have good table manners," he told her.

"Michael!" A smile tried to edge her lips, but she refused it.

"A man can't always eat alone. It's bad for the digestion," he said, his voice innocent.

"Michael." Her eyes turned soft and slightly worried. "Stop. Please."

Between them, Baby was still as a pebble. She clutched her ragged doll to her breathlessly. Michael could almost feel the energy of her hope radiate straight inside his soul, and the children in the back seat listening avidly.

"Guess I could go home and scrounge something to eat by myself," he complained pathetically and without shame.

"Maybe you could eat leftover peach pie." Bailey's gaze stayed relentlessly on his.

So she was jealous! That's why she wouldn't accept his offer. Well, he could fix that, too. "I sent it over to Gunner's. I am a thoughtful neighbor." His expression turned pitiful. "But I haven't been to the grocery in two weeks, and a man gets tired of canned soup three meals a day—"

"All right," Bailey interrupted. "I shouldn't reward your underhanded tactics, but...did you really send Deenie over to Gunner's?" She stared at him with hopeful eyes.

"Yes. He needed some glitter in his life, and I did not." He started the car. "Let's go get some pancakes."

The back seat exploded with noisy happiness. Michael smiled. He liked being the hero. He liked getting Bailey to give in. The indirect approach definitely worked with her.

He wondered how he could manage to keep her from going to Gunner's in the morning. Michael had sent Deenie and her peach pie to his rival; it seemed unnecessarily neighborly to hand over Bailey, too.

Maybe all this indirect approach was the right way to find out why Bailey had suddenly ceased her night-time visits to his bed. He glanced at her, but she was fussing with Baby's hair. Bailey still looked kind of peaked, which worried him. Her usually sparkly blue eyes seemed dimmed and tired. Maybe it was a womanly thing, a monthly function bothering her in some way.

Maybe she needed to go to the doctor, but couldn't because she didn't have the money!

Michael felt ill suddenly. If she needed to see a doctor, he'd carry her kicking and screaming and pay the bill himself. Maybe he should just directly ask Bailey why she'd quit coming around.

There was a time to be direct and a time to sidestep. He missed Bailey in his bed—and maybe he'd just best say so. Clear up any miscommunication on that matter they might have had.

Perhaps it would be even better to endure a month of Sundays hauling her flock to church.

Anything—including sticky pancakes with the numerous Dixon children—to get her upstairs and under the sheets with him again.

BAILEY KNEW it was a bad idea to go to the pancake house. It wasn't the tab alone that bothered her; it was knowing that she probably wouldn't be able to hold her stomach down. She'd had to leave during the service and hurry to the rest room. In all her life, she'd never been ill like this. It was like a flu she couldn't get over. At Gunner's she'd gotten sick from the aroma of sausage links and tacos, similar to the rich aromas in a pancake house. But she'd heard the gasps of joy over Michael's invitation—and there'd been no way she could deprive her siblings of such a treat.

She prayed for just one hour of calm sea.

"Howdy!" Deenie's father came to stand by their table with a big smile, eyeing their group with interest. "Brad, you've got yourself quite a gathering this morning."

"I do, Dan." Brad grinned at the man and motioned to a seat. "Sit down and join us for a cup of coffee."

"I'll do that. Deenie, grab a chair and sit yourself down so I can bend Brad's ear."

The momentarily calm sea rose in Bailey's stomach, threatening to pitch as Deenie looked down on all of them. She slid into the empty seat between Michael and Brad, staying far away from Bailey and the children.

"How's the collection coming along?" Dan Day asked.

"Fine, fine." Brad nodded and stirred his tea. "I'll be ready for the show. I think you'll be pleased."

"Show? What show?" Deenie halted her ogling of Michael and stared at her father. "Daddy, you're not doing a show for him, are you? You said you never backed starving artists, only ones with real talent." She sent a dismissive look around the table at the motley clan.

"Brad has real talent, Deenie." Her father lowered his brows at her. "You'd be surprised at his work."

The look on her face said she'd be shocked if he could paint with more than one primary color. Her mouth was wide open with distaste. Bailey didn't know how much longer she was going to be able to hold onto the love-your-brother homily she'd just en-

joyed in church. Pouring her water glass over Deenie's
hair-sprayed head wouldn't be loving, but watching
the hard-packed shellac turn into rivulets of glue
would be very satisfying. She bit her lip to keep from
snatching up the glass, though it was difficult when
Deenie's hand roamed over to Michael's.

"Everybody's doing their part to help the Dixons
with their tax problem," she said smoothly. "It's nice
of you to buy them Sunday brunch."

"Mind your manners, Deenie," her father commanded swiftly. "The whole town's offered to do craft
shows and bake sales to help them out, and Bailey's
turned 'em all down flat. I'm not doing this show for
charity. I'm doing it because it's gonna make me a
huge pile of frijoles. And I'm picking up the tab for
ya'll's meal today." He threw a hundred-dollar bill on
the table and waved Michael's protest off. "It's minor
compared to the money you're going to bring me at
the showing, Brad. Consider it a slight advance."

"Oh, Daddy." Deenie's tone was disbelieving and
demeaning. Clearly anything the Dixons had couldn't
be worth much.

"I've never seen an artist of Brad's talent. He's
worth showcasing. One day, you're going to see his
work in the most fashionable homes in Hollywood."

"Hollywood!" Deenie breathed. "I don't believe
it." But her gaze fastened on Brad with sudden, cal-
culating interest.

"I think your father's being a bit of a salesman,"
Brad said modestly.

She snapped her head around to stare at her father.
"Are you, Daddy?"

"Nope," he said simply. "My wallet started jumping the minute I laid eyes on Brad's work."

"Oh, my," she said in a silky whisper. "Daddy never does anything unless it's going to win big." Her eyes went doe huge on Brad as if she'd never seen him before. "Can you paint me?"

"Well—" Brad glanced at Dan hesitantly.

"I've always dreamed of Hollywood," Deenie said, pleading. "You could paint me in my best evening gown, with my Judith Lieberman sparkly shoes and my heirloom jewelry. I'd look like a movie star. Would you, Brad?"

Bailey lowered her eyes at Brad's predicament. Her stomach felt like it might heave any second. The children were all sitting quietly, staring at Deenie and big Mr. Day, who was smiling at his daughter as if she'd had an idea as bright as her silvery bleached hair.

Bailey felt a hand cover hers suddenly. She glanced up to see Michael mouth the words, "Are you all right?"

She nodded briskly, trying not to think how comforting and warm his skin felt on hers. He withdrew his fingers, and her shoulders sagged. Suddenly, the overwhelming combination of pancakes and eggs and sausage and Deenie's disdain washed over her in a tidal wave, prickling her skin with chill bumps and the panicked realization that she was going to be sick again.

"Excuse me," she blurted, leaping up from the table. She flew to the washroom, painfully aware of all the pairs of eyes watching her mad dash.

Ten minutes later, she collected herself enough to return to the table. Deenie and Mr. Day had departed. Michael stared at her in consternation. Brad looked away to save her from embarrassment. The children, well used to her frequent dives into a bathroom, barely looked up from the food they were eating.

Bailey knew she wouldn't make it through another minute in the pancake house. "Do you mind if I go sit in your car?"

Michael stood at once. "Of course not." He helped her into her coat and escorted her out into the bracing, fresh, crisp air. "Are you all right?"

She nodded weakly. "I'm fine."

"You're not fine." He opened the car door so she could slide in, then closed it and went around to the driver's side and got in. "You left church this morning, too. What's wrong?"

"Nothing. It's just something I ate, probably." The story she hadn't really been willing to tell Gunner didn't fall any easier from her lips now. Somehow she had to tell Michael the truth.

"You didn't eat *anything*." He brushed her hair from her face. "You're pale, Bailey. You need to see a doctor. I'm taking you over to Doc Watson's house right now and tell him he needs to take a look at you."

"No!" Bailey shook her head. "Don't disturb him on Sunday, Michael."

"He's a doctor, that's what he's for." Michael took a deep breath. "Let me run you to the emergency room, then."

"I'm fine. I already saw Doc Watson this week, anyway."

Michael looked at her suspiciously. "You did?" It was obvious he didn't believe her. "What did he say?"

"It's just a stomach flu." Now was not the right time to tell him the truth, so she could only hope that this little fib right after church wasn't going to do her chances for heaven serious damage. But she was more ashamed and upset than ever. Dread of his reaction dried her mouth. He certainly wouldn't be delighted with their predicament, that much she knew.

"You've had a stomach flu that's making you this ill for as many days as it's been since you've seen the doc." He shook his head. "Doc Watson's getting old. You could have something more serious, Bailey, like appendicitis or something."

"I don't!" she snapped. Ashamed, she shook her head. "I'm sorry. I didn't mean to bite your head off. I'd really just like to go home and lie down." She rolled her head against the headrest to look at Michael. His worried gaze went deep into her heart. She had to tell him soon, and the truth of what was wrong with her made her feel that much worse.

The Dixon family left the pancake house and tumbled into the car. Five little pairs of hands reached up to stroke Bailey's face. "Are you okay?" the children asked, petting her hair and her shoulders and every other part of her they could reach.

"You usually love pancakes," Beth pointed out with nine-year-old common sense.

"I know." Bailey closed her eyes. "I'm sorry I cut everyone's breakfast short." Especially the only time some of her siblings had ever been out for a meal.

"You didn't." Brad belted in the kids and himself. "We were almost finished, anyway."

"Bailey's been sick all week," six-year-old Amy told Michael, her blue ribbons bouncing importantly. "Her tummy's upset."

"Like a volcano," seven-year-old Sam informed him. "We watched a video of one in school, and that's exactly what Bailey erupts like." The freckles on his face were darker than Bailey's and smudged with syrup.

Eight-year-old Paul shook his head. "She's more like a geyser. They spew all the time." His tone was righteous with the superiority of greater age.

"She *erupts*," Sam insisted belligerently.

"Spews!" Paul stated authoritatively.

"Erupts!" Hating to be wrong, indignant because he was younger than Paul and stinging from Paul's know-it-all tone, Sam launched a sneaky fist at his brother.

"Spews! Bailey, Sam hit me!" Paul cried.

Bailey didn't see the hitting, but the back seat warfare made her want to slide under the floor mat.

Suddenly, all the well-behaved Dixon children were shouting, the din like loud surround-sound in a movie theater.

"Paul's looking at me!" Sam shrieked. "He's making those wolf fangs you told him not to!"

Baby began crying in the front seat. "I want my lamb baby!"

"Hey!" Brad tried to pin arms and separate bodies, but the commotion swelled out of control. Beth screeched at the top of her lungs, pressing against the car door to keep herself safe from flying limbs and starting to cry because her freshly ironed dress was getting mussed. Bailey was so weak she could only groan. She didn't want to move and risk the nausea returning. The smell of syrup and bacon clung to the occupants of the car, and with the uproar behind her, she seriously feared her stomach would have another heave of volcano or geyser proportions and illustrate Sam's and Paul's argument more vividly than they were.

"Enough!" Michael roared.

The car quieted instantly. Even Bailey rolled her head to stare at him. No one had ever heard Michael raise his voice.

"Now, if you can't behave—Paul, don't look at Sam—I won't take any of you with us the next time I take your sister out."

Bailey's lips parted. *Take me out? Is this a date?* It certainly sounded that way!

Apparently, Michael thought so, too. "Your sister and your brother," he amended quickly. "If you can't act like big people, you don't get to go with us. Got it?"

There was a chorus of yes, sirs, and the back seat remained quiet.

"Now. About your virus, which got this whole debate started, Bailey."

She felt Michael's gaze on her, questioning. "It's *nothing*," she reiterated.

"It's *something*. You're not skimping on going to the doctor because of money, are you?"

"No. I told you, I went to Doc Watson." She didn't dare look at him.

"I'm taking you home," Michael said, his voice strong and determined. "And I'm checking on you tonight, after I've done my chores. If you're not better, if you're not looking a lot more like the Bailey I know, I'm hauling you into Dallas to a first-rate physician."

She opened her mouth to argue, but he put a restraining hand on her leg. "I mean to have my way about this, Bailey. It doesn't do your family any good if you don't take care of yourself, and money shouldn't be an issue. You've rarely been sick a day in your life, but if one of my cows was as sick as you are, I'd be calling out the vet. And if you've been ill like this for a week, you need a good, thorough going-over by a qualified city doctor. In fact, I've got a good mind to call Doc Watson and tell him you need a prescription to get you on the road to recovery. I've got my cell phone with me, and—''

''Michael! Please just take me home!'' Bailey realized he was about to call Doc Watson. ''I promise I'll be better soon.''

He slowly turned off the cell phone. ''Okay. But much more spewing *or* erupting, and off you go. If the kids get sick with this bug, you're going to have a real mess on your hands.''

Bailey tore her gaze away from his. She had one. He just didn't know how serious the mess was.

Chapter Five

Bailey dove into bed as soon as they arrived home. She was too mortified to do more than mumble a hurried thanks to Michael. He was staring at her with such worry that she quickly made good her escape to the soothing safety of her bed.

When she awakened hours later, shadows were growing long and dark on the bedroom walls. February days were so short! Almost as if reminding her time was running out. She couldn't procrastinate much longer with what she had to tell Michael.

The thought made her weak with unhappiness. She did not want him to say he would marry her. Yet that was likely what the tough-to-tame cowboy would do. He had an honorable character.

But he would never be truly hers. If six months of sleeping with him hadn't brought them closer together, her distended stomach was certain to push them further apart.

She belted a pair of jeans, which still fit her snugly, pushed her head through an oversize sweater, pulled a hand through the long strands of hair, brushed her teeth and headed downstairs.

Her brother was working on a jigsaw puzzle with

the children. "I'm sorry, Brad," she murmured. "You could have used the good light of day to paint."

"Nope." He shook his head. "We've about got this puzzle whipped, and I'm determined to finish."

She picked up the box. It was a thousand-piece puzzle, and the scene wasn't well defined.

"Challenging," she commented.

"Yeah, but they'd graduated from five hundred pieces and wanted to go for tougher."

It was a good thing her mother had been fond of garage sales where she could pick up the board games and puzzles the kids loved for a song. Bailey smiled at the memory. "Any pieces missing?"

"The box wasn't opened. Nobody had even tried it."

She smiled at Brad's amazement that anybody in their right mind wouldn't enjoy such a pastime. Staring at the box, she shook her head at the number of pieces and the soft-focus scene.

She felt like she was in a puzzle with a lot of pieces and an undefined picture. "Michael said he was going to check on me tonight, but in the interest of keeping him from making a trip, I'm going over there."

Brad glanced at her. He hesitated when he saw the unhappy expression in her eyes. "Is it time?" he asked softly.

"I think it had better be. I wish it weren't, but he isn't going to buy the stomach flu story forever." She couldn't bear to see the worry in his eyes when there was nothing more wrong with her than morning sickness, which happened to plague her all day. How had her mother managed seven pregnancies? Bailey's throat felt raw and her middle bruised.

But her heart hurt the worst of all.

"Okay. You go on," Brad said, his eyes full of compassion. "Good luck."

She shook her head. It would take more than luck to make this conversation have a happy ending. She needed a miracle.

She swallowed convulsively. Maybe Michael wouldn't be home. Bailey shook her head at her cowardice. Then she'd wait for him. Briefly, she thought about Gunner's surprising revelation that he would marry her despite the child she carried. For an instant, Bailey closed her eyes. How she wished Michael loved her!

Outside, the late-evening shadows coalesced, combining their gloom to form winter's darkness. Why did February always seem to be the hardest, most chill month of the calendar? She climbed over the fence and cut across the wide Wade lawn to the side door used by the cowboys—and by her, when she slipped upstairs to Michael's bed.

There was no one in the kitchen. Most likely he was in the TV room. She hesitated, thinking that the cowboys might be in there with him. Maybe she should go home and call him instead. Glancing toward the phone, she saw the red blinking light and a number three. Either he was out or he hadn't come into the kitchen to check his messages. Easy enough to check the TV room and make certain he wasn't there. After that, she would know she'd been brave enough with her quaking determination and could throw up the white flag and retreat for the day.

To her surprise, the TV was on in the dark room. Bailey gulped as she saw boot heels hanging past the edge of the long leather sofa.

He *was* in. Lounging, like he was enjoying the peace and quiet. Bailey took a deep breath.

"Michael?"

The boots moved slightly after a second. "Hmm?"

"Can I talk to you for just a minute?"

DEENIE DAY widened her eyes. That blasted Bailey! How dare she usurp her plan? She'd been waiting for Michael to return for nearly two hours! Finally, she'd fallen asleep, knowing he'd come in and see her snuggled daintily on his sofa. What man could refuse a sleepy-eyed woman?

But now Bailey was here to spoil her carefully crafted surprise! She couldn't let her suspect that she was lying in wait. Doing her best imitation of Michael's grunt, Deenie hoped that would be enough to satisfy Bailey. Maybe she wanted to borrow butter or sugar to fix something for those wild orphans of hers, and a well-placed noise of assent might suffice.

Her body tensed. If Bailey turned on a light or came around the sofa, her plot would be ruined.

"Michael, I don't know how to tell you this."

Deenie heard the tears in Bailey's voice. Her eyes widened. Nobody cried over borrowing a cup of sugar! She shook her head. Bailey would. She had more pride than sense. Righteous little do-gooder, always spouting how she couldn't accept this or that. It made Deenie ill. She grunted again, hoping that Bailey would get on with it.

"I shouldn't have awakened you. I know you need your rest. But I think I like the darkness for what I have to say."

Oh, spit it out and disappear! Deenie's fingers curled into the warm afghan.

"I—I'm expecting a baby, Michael."

Deenie's mouth fell open. She held back a sarcastic snicker. Of all people, Miss Bailey Goody-Goody Dixon, pregnant! Going to church, elbowing in on Michael's charity at the pancake house, sending her brother out to sell his corny paintings—and she was pregnant! Obviously by some country lout who didn't want her, too, or she wouldn't be over here trying to wring something out of Michael. *Pathetic.* Deenie didn't dare move, she was trying so hard not to laugh.

"I—I just thought maybe you…"

Her voice drifted off. Deenie clutched the afghan tighter as she held in a giggle of malicious glee. Better-than-everyone-else Bailey was looking for a handout! And Michael was such a generous person, he would probably feel that he had to help a woman with six siblings and long, stringy hair.

Suddenly, the echo of running footsteps sounded in the hallway as Bailey hurried off. Deenie flung back the cover and sat up, peering over the sofa. "Well, well," she murmured, "guess she wanted more from Michael than pancakes. Tough luck!"

She sure wasn't going to tell him about the little beggar who'd come a-beggin'. In the future, though, she would have something to say whenever Bailey got that pious, we-mustn't-accept-charity look on her face. She truly was a Fallen woman now! Her father thought Bailey and Brad were such hardworking people who'd simply missed out on life's good breaks. They weren't. They were panhandlers preying on people's sympathy. It had hurt her feelings today when her father had reprimanded her to mind her manners about grungy ol' Bailey. Wouldn't he change his tune when she revealed the true Bailey to him?

That would put an end to the allowance dilemma she faced. *Daddy will have to quit threatening to cut back on my money once he learns the truth! I think I've heard all I'm going to hear about how I don't appreciate what I've got.*

Her father's threat had forced her on a full-scale marriage mission. She needed to marry the richest man she could in order to keep her in the style she loved. Gunner was nice, but Michael haunted her. He made her think about giving up her precious virginity, something a smart woman never bartered for less than a wedding ring.

Too bad Bailey hadn't known that. Michael probably would feel sorry for her, because in spite of his tough-guy demeanor, he was known to be a generous man. Almost to a fault. Bailey would know this as well as anyone. The fact that there had never been money in the Dixon household and that there was less now was widely known—if Bailey had tried to get a loan in Fallen she would have been turned down instantly. No doubt Michael would do the neighborly thing and offer to help his poor neighbor. Momentarily, Deenie felt a little sorry for Bailey. *No one's ever going to want her now that she's gone and gotten herself pregnant. She's ruined.*

But it wasn't Deenie's problem if Bailey didn't know that men would sleep with easy women but never marry them—so she dismissed it from her mind. *Deenie* had kept herself virtuous—and that was the kind of woman a man like Michael really wanted. Time and time again, she had heard it said that a man wanted only that which he had to work for, a challenge—and she presented a challenge, indeed. Michael would want her *badly*.

Smiling, she lay down to wait.

"I TOLD HIM," Bailey told Brad. Tears poured down her cheeks. "He didn't say anything!"

"Maybe he was stunned."

She melted into her brother's waiting arms. Her heart felt like it was breaking into a million pieces. "It was horrible!"

"I wish you'd let me talk to him, Bailey."

"No!" She shook her head vehemently against his chest. "No. I've made my bed, and...I suppose I must lie in it."

Brad had put the children to bed, so Bailey allowed the heartbreak and misery to pour out of her like a hard rain. All the worry and fear had drained her for so long she couldn't hold them in another moment.

"Oh, Bailey. I wish you hadn't fallen for him." Brad gently hugged her. "I can't bear to see you hurting this way."

"He was so nice this morning I let myself believe that he cared about me!" She still couldn't believe he hadn't said more than he had. But Michael could be gruff and monosyllabic. This morning's show of concern had obviously been for a situation he thought was temporary, a flu that required medicine. As he'd said, if she were one of his cattle, he'd be calling the vet out.

But a baby would be permanent. He'd been quite speechless over that.

"Why don't you give him a chance to take in what you just dropped on him, Bailey? After all, you've had a couple of weeks to adjust to the shock. He's probably sitting over there reeling."

Slowly, she backed away from her brother and

wiped her nose with a tissue he handed her. "I suppose you have a point. I was hoping for more—"

"And so you were disappointed when there was less. I know, Bailey." Brad's voice was kind. "I'd hoped for more, but quite frankly, if I were in his shoes, I think I'd feel like the floor had just given way beneath me."

"I wanted him to be happy," she whispered. "He's not happy."

"I'm not really surprised about that. He's been alone for so long that he's not given any thought to being any other way. Just because you've been keeping company with him doesn't mean he had more on his mind than that." Brad blushed to the roots of his hair.

What an example she was setting for her siblings! Her parents would be so disappointed in her. Mortified, she hung her head.

"Oh, Bailey. Don't let this upset you. It's not your fault, really." He tugged his sister's hair gently. "You know you wouldn't have gone there if our folks hadn't died. You took the full care of Dad on your shoulders, trying to push him into wanting life. You had a lot of responsibility I wasn't sharing." He cleared his throat. "I mean, it isn't wrong that you needed comfort, Bailey. It doesn't make you a bad person that you fell in love with the wrong man."

"I thought he was the right man," Bailey said softly, sinking into a kitchen chair. "My foolish heart wanted him to be so badly."

"You weren't thinking straight after Dad's funeral." Brad sat down across from her. "Bailey, suddenly you were looking at a big family that needed guidance. And had no money. If you grabbed a little happiness for yourself, I'll be the last one to say you were wrong.''

"Oh, Brad." She felt the tears trying to sting her eyes again, but she swiped at them resolutely. Crying wasn't going to solve the problem she faced. "Gunner asked me to marry him. He...he knows about the baby."

Brad leaned back in his chair. "You don't love Gunner."

"I know. But...accepting his offer would save this family a lot of pain."

"Let me know if you decide that's the course you're going to take. I don't want to be around when Michael finds out."

The thought was scary. Michael wouldn't have a whole lot of pity on her if she married his rival while pregnant with his child. "That wouldn't work very well, after all."

"Um, no. Take more than that whole pond we've got out back to cool those two off if you pit them against each other that way."

"I wasn't thinking to pit them," Bailey protested.

"I know. You're thinking of saving Dixon face, which is going to bring us fireworks and a hell of a lot of trouble." He patted his sister's hand. "Think of yourself for a change, Bailey. You love Michael. Give him a chance to come around before you give those two any reason to dig up the old feud."

She smiled slightly at her brother. "You're far more practical than I am."

"I'm not caught in the bind you are. It's easy to think through things when the heart isn't engaged." He grinned at her, obviously pleased to see her smile.

"I wish the right woman would come along for you, Brad. You deserve a good lady."

He glanced at his fingernails suddenly, which had speckles of blue paint and a line of navy under a nail. "I've already got my heart set on a gal."

Bailey's mouth dropped open. "Who? Since when?"

A rueful resignation spread over his face. "Deenie."

Bailey gasped. "Day? The Rodeo Queen?"

He nodded. "And to answer since when, since I intercepted her and her peach pie the other night."

WHEN MICHAEL GOT IN that night, he was tired and dirty. Clearly his ranch hands hadn't gone over every single inch of the fence rails as he'd instructed. He'd found one complete section down on the west side—wide open to the Dixon share of the watering hole. He shuddered to think of what might have happened if his steers had discovered it and decided to cause a ruckus next door. They were peaceful creatures as long as they didn't get spooked somehow—and there was plenty at the Dixon property to spook a man, never mind a steer.

He patched up the rails. Then he rode the full length of the Walking W to make certain no other rails were down. Tomorrow he'd grieve his useless ranch hands about their lack of industriousness.

Washing his hands, he ran warm water to get the chill out of his fingers, then toweled his face. He had his face in the paper towel when he realized he smelled something new, a scent decidedly feminine. Like perfume. Unless his cowboys had started wearing what they referred to as stink—cologne—he had him a female trespasser.

Bailey. Hope rose inside him. It wouldn't be like her to wear perfume, but maybe she'd run across some of her mother's. Perhaps—*oh, let it be so*—those crazy cowhands of his had been right, and Plan A was as simple as going to church if he wanted her in his bed.

The thought sent heat blazing through his body. Warm water couldn't take the cold from him the way Bailey could. He tossed the paper towel away and headed upstairs.

No Bailey.

He was disappointed. But he had smelled something quite unlike the leather and tobacco smells usually mingling in his home.

Maybe she was watching a movie while she waited for him. He hurried downstairs to the TV room.

"Howdy!" Chili, Curly and Fred chorused upon seeing him.

No Bailey.

"Howdy." He could barely keep the letdown from his tone. Glancing around, he saw no evidence that his woman had been here. Suspiciously, he sniffed the air, but the men smelled like…well, sweat.

"Thought I smelled something," he said gruffly.

"Smelled…something, boss?" Fred questioned. "Fire?"

He shook his head. "Never mind." Clearing his throat uncomfortably, he said, "I told Bailey I'd run by and check on her. 'Night."

Completely ignoring the chastising he'd meant to give them, Michael headed to the front door. The hour was growing late, almost too late for a social call. If he was crazy enough that he thought he was smelling

the woman, then it was time to get over there and
check on her as he'd promised.

Michael left, and the three cowboys shared a wink.

"Damn good thing we got here first," Chili said
with deliberate pleasure as he leaned back in the long
leather sofa.

"Yep," Curly agreed. "Otherwise he'd have found
more than perfume hanging around." He waved a
hand under his nose. "More like a skunk."

Fred started channel surfing. "Deenie sure did
scream when we lunged over the sofa at her. Some
frightening cuss words that little gal knows."

"Aw," Chili said, helping himself to the bowl of
peanuts Deenie had set out, as well as a bottle of wine
chilling in a bucket. "She who lies in wait in the dark
ought not be too upset when she gets ambushed better." He laughed. "Miss Fancy Pants wants herself a
cowboy, but she ain't gonna get him, is she, boys?"

"Nope," Fred and Curly agreed.

"BABY, IS BAILEY HOME?" Michael had hoped Bailey
would open the door, but Baby liked to greet everyone. The lamb bleated a welcome, too, dancing nervously on the worn hardwood floor.

"She's asleep," Baby said importantly.

"Is she feeling better?"

"Uh-huh."

He wasn't going to get more out of her than that.
Michael was discouraged, but he'd done what he'd
said. He had checked on Bailey, and if she was asleep,
best she stay that way. Maybe she was on the road to
recovery.

"She needs her rest," he said gruffly. "Thanks,
Baby."

"'Bye." Baby shut the door, and Michael walked down the bowed steps. Tomorrow Bailey started working for Gunner.

Suddenly, the piercing realization hit him that she wasn't ever coming back to his bed again. For whatever reason, Bailey had ended their relationship. She'd moved on. If he thought up enough excuses, she'd let him hang around her—the Dixons had never turned away any stray.

He wasn't a stray. If she didn't want him, then that was the way it had to be.

Even if it hurt like hell.

Chapter Six

"Plan A hasn't worked worth squat, I reckon." Chili gave the run-down Dixon house a desultory glance. "Bailey's spent the last week working for Gunner, and Michael hasn't done a thing to entice Bailey the way he oughta if he wants her back."

Curly shrugged and pushed his spectacles against his nose. "Michael hasn't figured out he's lost her, so he's not trying to get her back."

Fred Peters nodded. "He's kinda slow to wind up, in the womanizing department."

"Yep. Got a tin heart like his pa. Can't feel nothing deeply 'cause it strikes all the wrong notes." Chili rolled his eyes. "I'd never have said it while the old boss was alive, but damn, he was a mule. All that twisting and flailing Mrs. Wade did, believing he was in love with Polly Dixon. He paid his wife no mind at all."

"And he shoulda. 'Cause once she left, he dried up like a leaf blown off a tree." Curly scratched his nearly bald head under his hat. "Silly, if you ask me, to want a woman and not tell her so."

"I don't know how you teach a man to romance." Fred squinted at Bailey as she returned home from work and got out of her truck. "Seems like he oughta get off his duff and get busy with Bailey, rather than take it out on us. He's rode us harder than a rodeo bull for the last week, and I'm about to give out!"

"You've been giving out for the last thirty years," Chili commented. "We told him we'd take care of matters, and I s'pose a man's only as good as his word. It's time for Plan B."

"What is it?" Curly demanded.

"Hell if I know." Chili screwed up his mouth in thought. "But I still say sometimes it takes force to get two points to make a straight line."

"Seems to me a line could be real long, and that's not what we want," Fred pointed out with simplistic logic. "We want to force the two points *together*. Why, almost on top of each other so they form one large point."

Chili sat up. He snapped his fingers. "That's it!"

HORRIFIED, Bailey stared at the three cowboys precariously perched on the roof of her house, industriously pulling off wooden shingles. "What are you three doing? Why are you pulling off my roof?"

They halted and looked at her.

"You've got a bad roof," Chili intoned.

"Well, I know that! The whole house is falling down, but I can't afford a new roof. I'll be lucky to pay the taxes on this place, much less repair it." Bailey put her hands on her hips. "Doesn't Michael keep you busy enough?"

"Yep. But we gotta look after you, Miz Bailey." Curly clamped his hat down more tightly with determination. "Your folks always treated us like we was one of theirs. We can't let their family live under a bad roof. Ain't safe for the young 'uns, you know."

She paused at that. Of course she didn't want the children to live in an unsafe environment, but...

"Fred," she called suspiciously. "Did Michael send you to inspect my roof?" Fred was the most honest of the three, or perhaps he didn't camouflage his expression as well. If they were up to no good—and something about Chili's and Curly's deft answers made her wonder—Fred would likely spill the truth.

The cowboy muttered something, which was carried away by the breeze. She frowned. "Exactly what is wrong with my roof?"

"You've got roof worm, Miss Bailey."

"Roof worm!" Bailey narrowed her eyes at the sincerity in the cowboy's face. "I've never heard of those before."

"They're rare, ma'am. Usually make their nests in extremely old roofs 'cause the wood is tastier. Been seasoned longer. They'll eat holes right through like termites, only worse because they get real busy in the winter just when you want nothing more than to snuggle under warm covers indoors. And they kick up a powerful ripe smell in the summer when they're mating."

"Oh." The very idea made Bailey's stomach pitch.

"Your roof being wood makes it a terrible fire hazard, too." His watery blue eyes were focused in his lean face. "Your house being wood, too, why, ya'll are just living in an accident waiting to happen."

"And are you planning to brick my house, too?" she snapped, wondering how she was going to finance a roof. She might as well try to buy the moon.

"Say, now, there's an idea!" Fred said brightly. He

turned to Chili. "We got a buddy in the sand and gravel business. Bet he could get his hands on some—"

"Fred!" Bailey interrupted. "I wasn't serious. It was a question, not a…a suggestion." She sighed as more shingles landed with a loud crack on the ground. The pile of discarded wood grew larger as they resumed work.

Chili hesitated. "Bailey, I think Baby needs you."

"Why do you say that?"

"She just looked at me and said she needed to, um…go."

"How can you see her?"

"Well, I tore off this shingle, and there's a hole where the roof lining should be. Hole's big as a basket, and I can see right through."

It figured. "If there are huge holes you can see through," she said tightly, "how are we going to live in the house while you finish the job you so kindly began without asking me if I wanted a new roof!"

It should have been a question, but anger and desperation turned it into a shriek of sorts. They had no money for a motel room, no place to stay. And these well-meaning cowboys had just torn the roof off the only shelter she and the children had.

"Oh, you need have no care of that," Chili said airily. "The Walking W's big enough for all of ya'll, and all your first and second cousins, too."

Bailey snorted. "I'm sure Michael would enjoy having us under his roof."

"He said his *casa* was *su casa,* and that we was to do our utmost to secure your dwelling for ya," Curly informed her. "Under no circumstances are we to leave this house in any but the most safe conditions."

"I think my feelings about accepting charity are well-known." She gritted the words out.

"Oh, no, ma'am." Fred Peters pulled off his hat and placed it over his heart. "This ain't no charity. Michael did say that he owed ya'll much more money than he'd ever paid your father for the use of his watering hole. Michael said it was the only honorable thing to do."

The only honorable thing to do was to send his cowboys to build her a new roof. Bailey wanted to giggle hysterically. *And I was so worried he'd want to do the honorable thing and marry me! A new roof, even bricks he'd give me, but never his name.*

"All right," she said grimly, "if Michael wants seven Dixons living under his roof while he's instructed ours to be removed without consulting us, then the least we can do is comply graciously."

MICHAEL FELL into bed that night, glad for the peace and quiet after spending his day in the city haggling over the price of beef. With the summer's drought, he'd had to bring in extra feed and hay for his cattle, all at an inflated cost. He needed extra money to meet expenses, and it was a battle getting anyone to pay the higher beef prices. All the ranchers were telling the same story, but Michael found it wearing. He was in much better shape than a lot of ranchers because of the Dixon pond.

Thank heaven for that. He'd own many less head of cattle if he didn't have the blessing of Dixon water.

He closed his eyes and tried not to think about the Dixon woman next door, who was even more difficult to understand than big city folk.

"Baa! Baa!"

"Aiee!" Michael cried, jackknifing to a sitting position and startling the tiny lamb Baby had put on his bed. It let out an agonized bleat, but the little girl petted it, calming it down.

Michael wasn't calm in the least. "Baby, what are you doing here?" Belatedly, he thought to tug the sheet over his bare chest.

"I live here now," she said simply. "Me and my baby lamb. And my baby doll."

He raised a brow. "No, you don't, Baby," he said, struggling for a kind tone so he wouldn't upset her, no matter how much his heart felt like it might beat right out of his chest. "You live next door with your brothers and sisters."

"Uh-uh." Baby shook her head resolutely and got on his bed, perching with the lamb carefully hooked under one arm. It bleated again but didn't move away from the child who had adopted it. "We're gonna live with you from now on."

He didn't think so, not while he had any sense left in his head. The last thing he wanted under his roof was Baby and her lamb and her ragged doll, and all the noise and confusion Dixons brought with them. "Baby, you should go on to bed now." He made his voice gentle and reasonable. "You and baby lamb need your rest so you'll grow big and strong."

"Baby lamb isn't going to be big and strong," she pointed out sadly. "She's a runt. Nobody wanted her but me."

He didn't want either of them in his bedroom. "Baby, listen, why don't you—hey, why do they call you Baby, anyway? What's your name?"

She shrugged and patted her lamb. "My mommy always called me Baby. Oh-my-Lord-where's-the-baby and Oh-dear-heaven-check-the-pond-for-the-baby.''

"Oh, sweet Jesus," Michael muttered.

Baby straightened with a smile on her face. "And oh-sweet-Jesus-the-baby's-gone-again!''

He closed his eyes. *Like all the other Dixons, she's just cut out different.* "I'll bet Bailey wonders where you are," he hinted.

"Nope. She's asleep. And you told me not to wake her up.''

"Well, how about Brad? Maybe he's calling, Oh, dear heaven, the baby's gone again." He winced at repeating the absurd string of words, but he had nothing on under the sheet, and he was trapped by a precocious ragamuffin and her runt lamb, and there wasn't much more he could do than try to communicate at her level.

She stared at him. "Moving his paintings downstairs.''

Warning bells went off. Michael cocked his head to listen carefully to the tiny fount of information. "Downstairs...where?''

"In your house.''

"In my house.''

"Uh-huh.'' Baby nodded.

"Okay," Michael said carefully. "Why is Brad doing that?''

"Because the cowboys took the roof off our house and Brad doesn't want his paintings spoiled if it rains before the big show.''

"What cowboys took the roof off your house?'' Michael had a sinking feeling he knew. They'd said to leave everything to them—and he had—but they'd better not be behind this lamb and child making themselves comfortable on the foot of his bed.

"Mr. Curly, Mr. Chili and Mr. Fred," Baby said helpfully. "They're going to build us a new roof. They said we have to live here until they're finished."

His throat dried out painfully. He'd dreamed of Bailey spending the nights in his bed again, but...if Baby was saying what he thought, and she seemed pretty clear on her facts, that meant the entire Dixon band was in his home. He'd go crazy from the commotion and disarray of seven Dixons in his refuge, his sanctuary. He'd never be able to get Bailey under the sheets with all her siblings clinging to her. Seven Dixons and a lamb.

"I'm gonna kill them," Michael promised under his breath. "Those cowboys are gonna dream of retiring somewhere far from the Walking W ranch!" There was only one thing to do, and that was talk to Bailey. "Um, Baby, if you'll step out of the room for a second, I'll pull on a pair of jeans and we'll go find your sister."

"She's asleep."

"I know that!" He blew out a breath. "Baby, please go outside in the hall for one second, all right?"

"'Kay." She slid off the bed, carrying her armful of lamb with her.

Pulling the sheet with him, Michael jumped into the closet, practically skinning his legs on the zipper, he pulled his jeans on so fast. But he couldn't trust Baby not to pop in to check on him. He jammed his feet sockless into a pair of boots and jerked on a T-shirt that read I'd Rather Be Rodeoing, a present from Curly last Christmas.

"Okay, Baby, take me to Bailey."

He followed her through the hall and down the staircase to the east wing of the house. It was a minor relief that the cowboys had the consideration and presence of mind to place the Dixons as far away from him as possible.

But he was going to have to tell Bailey that there had been a mistake. Her brood could not stay with him. It would be catastrophic to his way of life.

Baby pointed to a guest bedroom. Michael nodded and stepped inside. All he could see in the moonlit path across the bed was a pile of blankets and two heads barely poking out. Swallowing, he moved to the side of the bed. Instantly, as if she slept uneasily in her surroundings, Bailey opened her eyes. Upon seeing him, she sat up.

Her worn cotton nightdress emphasized her shape under the white material. Breasts that were fuller than he remembered swayed sensually. Bailey blinked at him with a gaze that was concerned and cautious. She pushed back her hair, and her breasts moved enticingly under the fabric.

A barely clad Bailey was the last thing he'd expected. "Oh, my Lord," he breathed. Because that sounded so dangerously aroused, he muttered, "I found Baby."

"That's just what my daddy used to call me!" Baby beamed as she threw her arms around his leg, her little body standing on his boot like a lead weight. "Oh-my-Lord-I-found-Baby!"

"What's happening?" Amy sleepily sat up next to her older sibling.

"Go back to sleep," Bailey told her. "Baby got out of bed but she's back now."

"I couldn't sleep," Baby said, clinging to Michael.

Michael didn't think *he* would after seeing Bailey. He swallowed in a too-dry throat. He'd wanted Bailey in bed, but this bed was occupied by young children. One was solidly attached to the top of his boot. Everything was horribly awry.

And yet, in spite of this stunt—and he was still going to string up his cowboys for what they had done— something inside him was glad Bailey was in his house, especially wearing that thin nightgown. It was almost worth the trauma of suffering the other six Dixons.

And the lamb.

Then Bailey's long hair fell over her shoulder, curling against the sheet as she pulled Baby into bed beside her. The lamb found its nearby baby blanket on the floor, but Michael barely noticed. The length of pale silkiness shone in the dimness, tantalizing him with memories of how he used to have Bailey next to him under heaps of covers. She loved to sleep completely covered by blankets and always kept her nude body so tightly against his that he could feel every smooth, satiny inch of her. Burying his face in her long, soft hair was a pleasure he'd allowed himself to fully enjoy. His insides yawed with memory, pained by need. He felt his body responding in a way that would drive him crazy until he found sweet relief.

Obviously, there would be no relief. He cursed to himself.

Those damn cowboys had conjured up the worst possible hell he could suffer. Bailey next door and not coming to his bed was bad enough, but Bailey so close and yet completely unavailable was more mind-wrenching than he should have to bear.

He backed away from the bed and briskly nodded. ''Good night,'' he muttered before escaping.

Tomorrow he was going to have serious words with three semiretired hands who were a bit too efficient at stirring up trouble in the name of good intentions.

Chapter Seven

Michael avoided Bailey and the rest of the Dixons for the next five days by being gone long before sunup and returning well after the dinner hour, when he could grab some food and slink upstairs without running into any of them. The role of sociable host would be beyond him. Strangely, he didn't mind them in his home as there was no evidence they were actually in residence.

Out of sight, out of mind.

Except for Bailey. Thoughts of her plagued him night and day like a bad rash he wanted to scratch with furious abandon. From afar, he watched the progress on her roof with hopeful eyes, proud of the industriousness with which his ranch hands applied themselves. All the split, weather-beaten shingles came off. A black tarp was nailed into place.

Then all progress halted. He didn't think too much about it the first day, but by Saturday morning, when there was no sign of a fence-sitter atop Bailey's house, he went looking for them at the bunkhouse.

And found all three under blankets.

"Oh, no. You don't get a day off," he told them emphatically. They occupied different sofas and reclining chairs in the den where they could watch TV, covers pulled up to their chins. "Faking sick is not part of this plan. You three get up on top of that roof and finish the job. I never said I wanted Bailey moved into my house, so jump up and get to work so she can get out of my house."

"Don't reckon we can," Chili said, his voice a croak.

"We're under the weather," Curly said with a moan.

"Too much cold wind," Fred rasped, his nose snuffly. "We're sicker than we've been in all our time at the W."

Michael closed his eyes on an indrawn, impatient breath. Tension packed into his shoulder muscles as he struggled for control. "What about Bailey's roof?"

Chili wheezed as he sat up. His white mustache drooped over cracked lips. Eyes blazing with the stress of high fever peered woefully at Michael. "If you want us to work, we will. You're the boss." He broke into a fit of coughing, which doubled him over.

"You really are sick!" Michael exclaimed, hurrying to gently push Chili into a prone position. "How long have you been like this?"

"Since night before yesterday." Chili curled into a ball with a groan.

"Why didn't you call me?"

"We thought it'd pass. We didn't want to let you down with the plan, Michael." Chili closed his eyes. "Plan B was going so well." His voice drifted off.

Michael glanced around the room at the other two, who appeared just as ill. He hurried to refill their water mugs, which looked as if they hadn't had anything in them for a long time. "You should have called me."

"Didn't want to bother you," Fred said quietly. His face was flushed, and he seemed to be shivering under the blankets.

"So you'd rather die on me!" Michael shook his head and poured cold water onto worn washcloths, which he put beside each man. "Put that on your forehead. What have you been taking for the chills and temperature?"

"Ain't much here to take, Michael. We're never sick. And when we get a little bump or scratch, we run over to the Dixons'."

Curly put his wrinkled hands under his stubbly chin as he lay on his side. He looked childlike and frail, and suddenly Michael was worried. None of these men were young. They were fit, but it had been an extremely cold February.

"I'm calling Doc Watson," he said with sudden decision. "And if he decides you need shots in your rumps, I'm going to insist he use his biggest needles. It'll be just reward for the three of you wallowing down here in your misery without letting me know. And you left me stranded up there in plenty of misery of my own, so you've brought all of this on yourselves."

For a moment, interest stirred the cowboys' eyes open. "How's Plan B going, anyway?" Chili asked with a ghost of a grin.

Michael scowled. "As I said, I'll insist on the most painful needles Doc Watson can bring."

The three hands closed their eyes and groaned as Michael slammed the door behind him.

"I believe he means it," Fred said apprehensively. "I hate shots."

"I wish Michael weren't so much like his pa. He's

getting more ornery all the time,'' Curly said pathetically.

Chili threw an arm over his forehead before snatching up one of the cool cloths Michael had left. ''When Michael learns of our ancillary maneuver to Plan B, ornery just ain't going to be the end of it. We might as well just go ahead and expire right now and save ourselves the bodily injury!''

They all moaned again.

DEENIE KNEW one thing—her time to win Michael was running out. Her father was determined she become a worthy and responsible citizen, and she thought that very likely would trim her budget beyond what she could live on.

Through the grapevine, she'd heard Michael's loony ranch hands were down with some terrible flu. He'd been in Fallen asking after temporary help, even a nurse for the cowboys.

She could offer to nurse them, except after their awful prank on her the other night, she'd rather see them suffer as opposed to get well. Volunteering for the nursing job, even to earn Michael's gratitude, wouldn't advance her cause.

However, the hands being stuck at the bunkhouse meant they wouldn't be in Michael's house. So she heated another pie—this one a blueberry her mother had put up last summer—and decided there was no time like the present to teach that cowboy just how much he'd enjoy eating sweet things from her fingertips.

Deenie smiled and pulled the zipper on her knit sweater a little lower so that her own sweet things were more visible to the casual eye. Even a stonyemotioned man like Michael couldn't fail to miss what she was offering.

Parking to the side of his house, she was glad she'd waited until after dark to arrive. He should be relaxing after a hard day of work. She could massage his shoulders! She crept in the side door and hesitated in the kitchen. There were no dishes in the sink to indicate he'd been home to eat supper, but then, Michael was very tidy. No smell of cooked food lingered in the air, but maybe he'd just grabbed a snack.

He'd be ever so grateful for her dessert. Smiling, she artfully laid the pie on the table, placing two napkins and two forks beside it, in a hint he'd be too much of a gentleman to refuse.

When she heard boots on the wooden floor behind her, Deenie smiled with pleasure. Slowly, she turned, the inviting smile instantly disappearing. "Brad! What are you doing here?"

"Mmm, mmm," he said appreciatively. "Deenie, I can't believe you brought me another pie."

"No!" she yelped, putting her hands out to halt his advance on her hard work. "Brad, it's not for you!"

"I say finders, keepers." He leaned over her and stuck his finger into the pie, breaking the beautiful crust as he brought up dripping blueberry sauce. Putting his finger into his mouth, he closed his eyes. "Oh, Deenie, it's delicious. You shouldn't have."

"I didn't!" She beat furiously at his chest. "You oaf! You've ruined Michael's pie!"

His eyes laughed at her. Furious, Deenie registered that Brad was a lot taller than she had noticed. He smelled good, too. But he had to quit stealing her pies! "I would never bring a pie to you. Don't you ever do that again!"

"Oh, Deenie. You hurt me. You really do." He stared at her. "Maybe you brought me something else, then?"

"I don't *think* so. I wouldn't bring you a glass of cold water if you were in Hades," she stormed.

He snapped his teeth together in the air as if he were about to take a bite out of something. "All I want is a little slice of what you brought," he teased.

"You're disgusting." But she couldn't help thinking that she liked a man who refused to back down. She'd never seen this confident side of Brad before.

But he was still a Dixon, a hand-to-mouth artist the tax men were after.

"What if I told you," he said in a confidential tone, "that I believe I'm already roasting in Hades, and that you're the only cold thing nearby? You are *cold*, Deenie Day."

"I can't believe how you're talking." Deenie was shocked by the new tone in Brad's voice. Almost as if he were trying to romance her. But she would never allow that. Not even if he did have the bluest eyes and the longest, most artistically untidy hair she'd ever seen on a man. It lay against the nape of his neck in disarray, marking the edges of a strong-chinned face. "Don't you ever cut your hair? It's a mess," she said scathingly. She had to ward him off. He was standing way too close for her comfort. The heat of his body prickled her skin.

"I don't have any money," he said, reaching out to touch her hair with one hand. "I cut the kids' hair, and I trim Bailey's."

"No wonder it's such an unstylish mess," she snapped.

"Maybe you'd like to cut mine for me," he suggested softly, picking up her hand and placing it on the back of his neck.

Against her will, her fingers ran through the strands briefly. "Never! I don't do anyone's hair, and rarely my own."

"It's too stiff," he said, touching her hair once again.

She slapped his hand away. "Too stiff for what?"

"To be natural. It's got more support in it than my pier-and-beam house."

"How *dare* you?" She wasn't going to allow a ragged Dixon to insult her. "You'd better get out of here before Michael catches you."

He drew a little nearer, and Deenie bent back over the chopping block table in the center of the kitchen. "I think you're the trespasser here."

She could feel his heat nearly searing the delicate no-zone of her femininity. No one had ever gotten that close to her before. She was to be seen and not touched. She teased, but she never satisfied—it was the only way for a woman to get what she wanted from a man. Unsettled, Deenie reached up to push Brad away with one hand. "Michael likes it when I bring him something."

"I don't think so." A slow smile moved Brad's lips. "I think you like bringing Michael things. I think *he* couldn't care less."

Outrage drew her firmly against the length of his body. She gave him a little desperate push. "You are horrible!"

As she pushed, he caught her wrists in his hands. "But I sure do like your pie, Deenie."

And then he kissed her. He kissed her long and slow and deliberately, and though she told herself she strug-

gled, Brad's hands never tightened as he held her to
him.

*I'm going to slap him so hard he sees stars. I'm
going to tell my daddy!*

The kiss ended suddenly as Brad pulled away, and
Deenie's eyes snapped open.

"I can't wait to paint you," Brad said huskily. "I'm
going to paint you just the way you are."

Deenie's insides raced. Her heart beat wildly with
excitement. It hadn't hurt to allow Brad one little kiss,
had it? She'd heard that artists painted most brilliantly
when they were intimate with their subjects. Well,
now he'd kissed her, so he ought to be able to capture
her beauty spectacularly.

"Make it big," she told him. "Make it the biggest
painting Fallen has ever seen. I want it so big even
Hollywood hears about it."

He smiled at her, his eyes on her lips, admiring. "It
will be my pleasure."

Unsure of his easy compliance to her demand, she
glanced away for a moment. He sounded so...so unlike Brad. Or at least the Brad she knew.

"Well, good." She tugged down her sweater and
jerked the zipper higher as his gaze seemed to be interested in that which she'd intended for Michael's
viewing. "I'll take this with me even though you ruined it—"

His hand locked on her wrist as she reached for the
pie. She halted, her gaze caught by his. He stroked her
arm in a mesmerizing gesture, and her hand relaxed a
little.

"Leave it. I'll think of you when I have my midnight snack, Deenie."

She jerked away from his caressing voice and his

strangely hot gaze and his stroking, which felt so good. "Don't bother to ever think of me!"

"How can I paint you if I don't? Haven't you ever heard how obsessed artists are by their current work of art? They immerse themselves in their subject."

Her vanity caught in that snare, Deenie decided she didn't have a stinging comeback to put him in his place. She wanted him to focus on her beauty so that the painting of her was the centerpiece of his show. If he was as good as her daddy claimed, she wanted to be the best he had. But she didn't want this dirt-poor Dixon *really* thinking about her. Surely he could paint her without making her feel as if he was devouring her like he would her pie.

She scurried to the door. "Will you tell Michael I was by?"

He grinned, closing in on her again. "Perhaps."

She edged her hand to the doorknob. "Will you at least save him a piece of pie?"

"I doubt it."

Furious, she flung open the door and hurried into the darkness.

"Next time you feel like making me dessert, I've got a mighty hankering for a chilled strawberry pie, Deenie!"

His laughter goaded her into slamming the door of her Mercedes convertible. He *could* burn in Hades for all she cared. *Never* would she make Brad Dixon anything—except miserable!

BAILEY WAS STILL UPSET enough with Michael that avoiding him was easy. A roof was not what a typical man gave a woman who was expecting his child. She knew he was keeping out of her way, too. It would be smart for him to continue doing so until her house was fit to live in again.

Gunner avoided her, too. He'd kept to his word— he was gone all morning while she worked in his office, leaving her paycheck on the desk for her to find every week.

Then she returned to her new home at Michael's. It was an odd arrangement. One man had offered to marry her and had given her a job. One man was the father of her child and had given her a roof and temporary sanctuary.

She had the strangest sensation she belonged nowhere but was simply balanced in between. Brad continued shuffling the children to school in the mornings; she picked them up in the afternoons. He had happily set up a makeshift studio in Michael's dining room, which he said had excellent light due to the large windows. His show was in two weeks, and whatever he was working on was big, requiring the largest canvas she'd ever seen him use.

Between his fervor for his new work and her unnerving sense of displacement in her life, Bailey stayed out of Brad's way. She could handle her own worries, particularly as the morning sickness had finally passed. For that, she was grateful.

So grateful that she could focus on other people's problems, and right now, Chili, Curly and Fred had their share. Brad had mentioned that all three were ill, but skinny, kindhearted Fred the most. Doc Watson was worried his fever indicated a more serious infection. If Fred didn't improve soon, Doc was going to have him admitted to a hospital.

Bailey pursed her lips with sympathy. She couldn't go down to the bunkhouse for fear of catching what they had, but she could make them a huge pot of chicken soup. Michael had mentioned briefly to Brad that he had to go into town for food for his hands.

He could be so considerate, Bailey mused as she stirred the broth. The aroma rose in a comforting steam, something she couldn't have tolerated a week ago. She closed her eyes, relaxing in the unexpected joy of cooking in Michael's kitchen. The hand she wasn't stirring with sneaked to her abdomen. A swell had begun to round her stomach. She'd taken to wearing her shirts untucked so they covered the zipper of the jeans she was no longer comfortable zipping.

It felt so good to be in the warmth and security of Michael's house during this cold, bleak February. Her baby must be thriving in the comfort of cozy solitude Bailey found herself enjoying.

The kitchen door opened and Michael strode in, carrying a large sack of groceries. "Hi."

His tone said he hadn't expected to see her, or maybe it was that she was cooking in his kitchen.

"Hi," she returned shyly. "I thought I'd make up some chicken soup for the cowboys. Brad told me they weren't feeling well."

He stared at her, his dark hair ragged and windblown. His eyes seemed bluer from the rough ruddiness of his cheekbones. Bailey swallowed. "I hope you don't mind."

After a moment he turned and put the sack on the chopping block. "You should be resting."

"Why?"

He shot her an impatient glance. "Because you're sick."

"I'm not sick, Michael. At least not anymore." She bowed her head and stirred faster.

"That's good."

His tone was noncommittal as he put away the groceries. Bailey frowned.

"Michael, I have to ask you…I mean…" Her voice drifted off. Did he intend for there to be nothing more between them? Was fixing her house the kind of support he intended to provide for his child?

"How's work at Gunner's going?"

She was startled at his question. "Fine. Why?"

"Just wondered."

He kept the back of his head to her as if her answer meant little to him, but she sensed that wasn't the case. Did he feel like she was cheating on him somehow? "I never see him, Michael."

"Oh."

She was beginning to get impatient with his lack of communication. She put the spoon on the spoon rest and went to stand beside him so he'd have to look at her. "Michael, why are you being like this?"

"Like what?"

"Uncommunicative."

He looked confused. "I thought I was saying a lot."

"You haven't said *anything*."

"Well I have," he began defensively. "We talked about your chicken soup. I said that was nice of you to do. I want you to relax and take care of yourself so you won't relapse, but you're determined to do everything yourself. I asked about your new job, and if you'd given me a chance, I was about to ask what luck you're having with the tax situation."

He finished all that with a glare.

Okay. So he found talking about the pregnancy awkward. Bailey understood that. Still, wasn't there something they should discuss, some rules they should agree on for raising the child?

By the stiff set of his posture, Bailey supposed not. Not right now. She lowered her head.

He tipped her chin with his finger. Hope flooded into her body at the warmth she saw in his eyes.

"I just don't want you overdoing."

"I won't."

"You're always doing for everybody, Bailey. While you're in my house, you're not the cook, you're not the maid. I want you to put your feet up and do nothing. The few hours you have to yourself between when you're done at Gunner's and before the children come home from school, you should just sit."

Her veins hummed as he moved his finger from her chin to stroke her neck.

"I don't mind you here a bit," he said gruffly.

She smiled.

"Thought it'd be terrible at first." He cleared his throat. "Didn't reckon you'd want to be here."

Bailey's lips parted. "Why did you have the roof pulled off my home if you didn't think I'd want to stay here?"

Michael pressed his lips together as he thought how to answer. How much of himself could he lay out, knowing the sting of rejection was nearby? She'd quit coming to his house at night. *She'd* quit coming to *him.* He had never, ever thought she'd cease her visits. No, he hadn't dreamed the cowboys would do what they had, but they'd forced her into returning to him. Michael secretly admired Plan B for its sheer audacity, though he would never tell them so. "I didn't know they were going to do it," he said honestly.

"They said you'd instructed them! That you said we could live here until the roof was finished."

"Well—" If he wasn't careful, Bailey's sense of pride would be offended and she'd walk out. He didn't want that! At least, he didn't want her pride offended. And if the truth were to be known, he was happy she was in his house. "You were always welcome here, Bailey," he said huskily.

She stared into his eyes, waiting.

And because he didn't know what else she wanted to hear, he did what he really wanted to do since she'd stopping coming to his bed weeks ago. He lowered his lips to hers, gently telling her that she was still welcome in his home. Even with the children and the lamb. He kissed her like a man drowning in sheer heaven. Hot emotion swept through him when she put her arms around his neck and surrendered to the kiss she'd initially held back from. He'd felt her reticence, but it was gone now. She returned his kisses as slowly and sensually as if they had all the time in the world to stand in the warm kitchen and keep the world outside where it belonged.

Briefly, Michael wondered how he could let Bailey know that she was welcome to *all* the rooms in his house. That the distance between her bed below and his bed upstairs was much shorter than when she'd had to cross their properties.

The side door swung open, shattering the spell. Instantly, Michael and Bailey jumped apart. A tall, elegant woman with silvery gray hair entered on a blast of freezing air. Michael's eyes went wide. "Mother?"

"Hello, son. You needn't sound like I'm a nightmare you've just awakened to, though from your tone I can tell you weren't expecting me." She gazed at him steadily, then slowly eyed Bailey from toe to head, settling, it seemed, on her lips. Nodding as if she'd seen all she needed to, she set a large suitcase on the floor with a thump. "Now what's this I hear about you needing a chaperon?"

Chapter Eight

Michael was so stunned he couldn't move. Bailey poked him purposefully. He walked forward to awkwardly kiss his mother's cheek. With his mother's appearance came all the resentment and feelings of abandonment he'd felt as a teenager—he didn't want to remember any of that. "If you drove all the way out here because you thought I needed help, you made a trip for nothing."

"Not help necessarily, Michael. A chaperon."

"I haven't needed someone watching out for me in years." He was annoyed by her insistence on the protective term. *And not when I was a teenager, when you were nowhere to be found.* A frown wrinkled his brow. "Someone misinformed you. If you heard that in town, I let it be known I was looking for a temporary nurse and maybe some ranch hands. Nothing you could help with."

His mother shook her head and allowed Bailey to take her coat. He wished Bailey wouldn't settle his mother in. She wasn't staying.

"No, I wouldn't be a qualified nurse or a good ranch hand. I'm here in the official capacity as chaperon."

"Says who?"

"Chili, Curly and Fred." She smiled her gratitude at Bailey as she proffered a hot cup of tea.

"What do they have to do with anything?" Michael demanded. Bailey could cease her hostessing now, he thought sourly. His mother was going right back where she belonged. She'd had her chance to provide a stable household of love and warmth. She'd blown it.

"They called and said that since they were sick, they couldn't provide their presence as proper chaperons. They asked me to come." Bailey was the recipient of another of his mother's warm smiles. "They were worried, and rightly so, that there might be talk."

"There'll be talk just by you being here," Michael growled.

"Michael!" Bailey protested.

He stared at her, his gaze steel enough to silence her—if she could be silenced.

"You must consider Bailey's reputation," his mother continued, ignoring her son's harshness. "And the children's. It's all fine and good for you to fix their roof. I think that's a wonderful thing to do. But in the meantime, we mustn't ruin the kind deed by giving gossips a reason to disparage the good Dixon name."

"Disparage the good Dixon name?" He didn't want to hear this. He didn't want to see her point. Heat under his collar reminded him uncomfortably that he'd never given one second's thought to Bailey's reputation.

Bailey stared at him like he'd sprouted an extra head. If he had, he hoped it would help him understand the fast-moving dilemma he found himself in. His goal had been to figure out how to return Bailey to his bed. The fence-sitters were supposed to assist him.

They'd sabotaged him. And with his mother, of all people! By the anger in Bailey's eyes, he knew she'd misread his remark about the good Dixon name. "There's no reason for anyone to ever question the fine Dixon name," he stated. "Bailey and I are not..." He faltered at the questions in Bailey's eyes.

"Are not what, Michael?" his mother asked.

"Are not...are not doing anything anyone would want to talk about," he finished in a rush. Had he saved himself? Were those the right words to soothe Bailey? Was his mother satisfied enough to return to wherever she'd come from?

Bailey lowered her chin. His mother glanced at each of them. "I see," she murmured. After a moment, she said, "It's not really a matter of whether anything's been done. My presence will make certain that no one suggests that it might have been." Stirring her tea, she waited for a reaction from him. Bailey stood at the stove, her eyes downcast.

"All right." He jammed a Stetson on his head and shrugged into his wool-collared jacket. "Not that I remember anyone in this house cared what gossips thought when you decided to leave, Mother. But if you think Bailey needs a chaperon, I'm sure you'll do your job. You can bet I'm going to make certain that a roof gets on the Dixon house pronto—if I have to hire a round-the-clock work crew to get it done. I wouldn't want to trouble you any longer than necessary."

He couldn't look at Bailey. If it wasn't for her roof, her siblings and her lamb, his mother wouldn't be here stirring up old pain. He hadn't seen his mother since his father's funeral, and no doubt she'd only attended to give his father a big fat raspberry and a magnanimous send-off to hell. Michael couldn't believe she was here. It was way too late for her to start acting like she gave a damn. He'd hire the fastest crew in town to get a roof on that falling-down Victorian money pit, send Bailey and her overflow home and his mother packing.

But right now, he was going to kill three meddling cowboys who'd forgotten whose side of the fence kept them fed, sheltered and employed. "*Chaperon,*" he muttered in disgust. "They're going to wish they'd never heard the word!"

"WELL, THAT WENT about as well as expected, I suppose."

Bailey met Mrs. Wade's eyes with difficulty. She was mortified by the way Michael had acted toward his mother! Clearly, he wasn't worried about Bailey's reputation, but shouldn't she have suspected he'd feel that way when he never said word one about the baby? "I think he was just surprised, Mrs. Wade," Bailey offered, knowing that wasn't the truth.

"Please call me Cora." The older woman winked at her. "Michael never was one for change or surprises of any sort." She laughed softly, remembering. "You sure have changed a lot since I last saw you."

Heat blazed across Bailey's cheeks. "Have I?"

"My, yes. Even prettier, if that's possible. Maybe a little taller. You might be putting on a bit of weight, which is flattering." She cocked her head at Bailey. "How've you been getting on without your folks, dear?"

She wasn't certain how to answer. She'd heard the ridiculous rumors that Michael Senior had been half in love with her mother, Polly. And that one day Cora had taken her broken heart down the road before she

got any more hurt by her husband's lack of regard for
her. A haunting image of herself in Cora's shoes
taunted her momentarily. Was Michael any easier to
know than his father had been?

"I sure did think about you when I heard your ma
had taken sick," Cora said softly. "I'm sorry you lost
your folks. They were fine people."

Bailey nodded, looking away so the sudden tears
that jumped into her eyes could stay hidden.

"Sherman King and my husband would have spent
their whole lives trying to destroy each other if it
hadn't been for Elijah and Polly keeping peace in the
middle. I know you miss them."

"I do." Tightness choked her.

"I hope Michael is being the gentleman he should
be to help you, Bailey. We owe your family a lot."

She gulped. "I—" What could she say?

Cora sighed. "You're still in love with him after all
these years, aren't you?"

"Yes, ma'am," she whispered painfully.

"Ah, well." Cora exhaled a regretful breath. "I'm
not the one to be much help cracking the code on a
Wade male." She was silent for a few moments.
"Running shy of the lasso, is he?"

Bailey barely nodded.

"His pa was darn stubborn. I don't suppose Michael's much different."

"I've been called real stubborn myself."

A slight smile touched Cora's mouth. "Hanging in
for the long haul, are you?"

"Until I'm convinced it's time to go on," Bailey
admitted.

"I wish I'd had an ounce of your gumption. My
marriage always felt like so much sand being sucked

out from under my feet by waves I never saw coming. It was easier to just move myself than get washed away.''

She sipped her tea thoughtfully, maybe even wistfully. Bailey squeezed her hands together and took a deep breath. ''I think your being here might be more help than you realize.''

''Oh?'' Cora glanced up eagerly. ''Michael wouldn't share your opinion.''

''No, but as you pointed out, Michael doesn't like to face anything he chooses not to,'' Bailey said with determination. ''Maybe it's going to take facing you for him to be able to want more from me than he does right now.'' She felt a burning blush rise to her face. There was no reason to say more. It was up to Michael and her to resolve how they were going to deal with the baby they were expecting.

MICHAEL SENT the bunkhouse door flying open. He strode to the den where the fence-sitters lay pitifully, propped on pillows, their faces pasty. Fred still looked worse than any of them. Michael nearly softened as he looked at the men, but then he thought about what they'd done to him and got angry all over again. ''One of you is about to draw your final paycheck at the Walking W. Which of you had the bright idea to call my mother?''

Three age-lined right hands raised immediately into the air. Michael paused, then crossed his arms. ''I might have guessed you'd present a united front.'' He shook his head. ''You were supposed to help me, not hinder me.''

''Hinder you from what?'' Chili asked.

What indeed? He'd merely asked them to help him

keep Bailey from going over to Gunner's side for good. He hadn't confessed to his underlying desire to have her back in his bed. "Hinder me from working." He gritted out the words.

"Ah, your mama's not going to bother you on the ranch. She's there for Bailey," Curly said.

"Bailey. Why does Bailey need anyone?"

"She needs to keep her reputation unsullied." Fred struggled to sit, his eyes glassy with fever. "We agreed to help her see your good points, boss, not to help *you* see any of *her* points you oughtn't be seeing without benefit of a wedding ring and a preacher."

He felt mildly irritated by that dig. "How do you know that would interest me?"

Chili blew out a sarcastic breath. "The only one who hasn't figured out how you feel about that li'l gal is *you.*"

"You ain't being fair to Bailey," Curly remonstrated.

"Fair!" Michael was really getting steamed. "Since when is it a crime to...to live next door to a woman and say hello every once in a while? Does that mean I have to propose to her?"

"You're trying so hard to fool yourself that you may have actually done it." Fred stabbed a meaningful finger at him before falling back on the pillows. "But you cain't fool us. As far as we're concerned, Bailey needs a chaperon. You can't just ruin her reputation and then go around bellyaching that everyone in Fallen, Texas, is misunderstanding the situation."

"You are!"

"You've taken her to church. And to Miss Nary's Pancakes and Dairy. Now she's living in your house.

For heaven's sake, son, what do you think people are gonna think?'' Chili demanded.

"That she needed a new roof!" Michael nearly shouted.

"That ain't what they're gonna say." Curly hit the mute button on the TV.

Michael eyed his ranch hands steadily, taking deep breaths as he studied them. "You three trapped me."

They were silent.

"You planned this. You said take her to church. So I did. Then you tore off her roof and moved her into my house. Now you've called my mother, who has been a disappearing act for years, and moved her in, which is going to call attention to the Walking W in a big way." He watched their faces for any sign of guilt, but there was none, which shook him just a little. Could it all be so coincidental? He didn't trust his three ornery employees for a minute. They lay around with their faces inscrutable and their eyes shuttered, but he had them figured out. "I guess what you want is for me to marry Bailey. Is that the result you're looking for?"

"Maybe it ought to be the result *you're* looking for," Chili returned.

Fred coughed, his chest heaving with the effort. "I never thought I'd say this, but I'm ashamed. I've always been proud to ride for the Walking W brand, but it no longer means what it used to." He coughed again. "You've threatened us more than once with letting us go. You need not threaten me again. I'll be packing my bedroll and heading out at the end of this week."

"Fred!" Chili and Curly exclaimed.

Michael's eyes narrowed. From the cowboys' reaction to this announcement, if there had been a script, it had clearly been deviated from. Fred appeared to mean every word.

"You can just go on." Fred waved his hand at his boss and turned toward the pillow. "I'll not be troubling you further."

Michael clamped his back teeth hard so the shock he felt wouldn't spread over his face. Curly and Chili stared at their very ill friend in dismay, no longer paying the least attention to Michael.

Michael nodded. There was nothing else to say. Slowly, he walked to the door, turning before he opened it. "I'm not the bad guy you think I am. I'm aware that I have feelings for Bailey. Trouble is, *she* left *me*."

Unable to say more, he left the bunkhouse, quietly closing the door behind him.

"Has the fever burned up your brain?" Chili demanded of Fred the instant Michael exited.

"I don't care if it has." Fred's pitifully thin voice lacked strength.

Chili and Curly glanced at each other with alarm.

"Are you feeling okay?" Curly asked, getting up to touch his friend's forehead.

"I feel better than I have in days. My conscience is at peace."

"Your retirement is in peril! You deviated from our plan and waved a red flag at Michael he felt forced to accept outta pride!" Chili took a deep breath. "What got into you?"

Fred sat up, his eyes no longer glassy but focused. "A vision. I had a vision last night."

"You had a what?" Chili and Curly stared at him, agog.

"It was," Fred continued, not paying them any mind, "the most frightening, most humbling thing that has ever happened to me in all my years. To be visited by those who have gone over before rattled my heart in my chest and brought to light the real big picture."

"What in blazes are you jabbering about?" Chili grabbed the prescription pill bottle Doc Watson had left, eyeing the label and the contents. "Did you snarf too many of these?"

"No." Fred lay back against the pillows weakly. "The worst of the fever hit me last night, baking me like a potato in its jacket. And suddenly, Polly and Elijah were right here." He pointed to the end of the blanket where his sock-clad, mismatched feet poked out. "They said they knew we was trying to do good, but that we were all wrong to assist Michael the way we have, when all he's got on his mind is..."

"Getting the milk for free." Chili was blunt.

"Exactly." Fred glanced toward heaven hurriedly. "Not that Bailey is a cow or anything."

"No!" The other two men glanced toward the ceiling in case Fred was getting another vision.

"Polly and Elijah said that Michael should marry her and make her his wife proper. Instead of doing all this slipping around, which we knew was going on, though we thought he would eventually see the light and propose." Fred sighed raggedly. "They say Michael ain't gonna see the light."

"Never?" Chili was horrified.

"Ever?" Curly's eyes bugged below his bald forehead.

"Not the heavenly light, idjit! The light, the real deal, the major clue. Michael isn't ever gonna perceive it as long as Bailey's slipping in and out of his bed.

We gotta keep Bailey outta his bed until he marries her. No hanky-panky while wearing an engagement ring, either. He's gotta do the deed right. He's gotta do it all the way. And," Fred finished with a flourish, "he's gotta do it of his own free will and desire. He's gotta make an honest man of himself willingly."

The men were silent for a long time.

"So you see why I didn't have any compunction about quitting the Walking W," Fred finally said. "We can't help him. Quite frankly, it pains me knowing up front that Michael's not going to do right by Bailey. Polly and Elijah are right. He's had the benefit of their daughter before marriage. He oughta pony up or leave her be." Fred stared at his two friends. "And we all know he ain't gonna leave her be. He's like a dog with a bee sting on its rear. He's gonna work and work at trying to get to it so he can get the relief he wants, but no matter how hard he tries, he ain't gonna be able to reach that far." He sighed heavily. "The fever was burning so hot, I thought I was dying! And I promised Polly and Elijah that if I wasn't laying on my very deathbed, I'd do my best by their daughter and their family. I just couldn't head into the great ranch in the sky without coming back to tell ya'll we've been working this dogie the wrong way."

"Heck fire!" Chili pulled at his long white mustache. "I wish you *had* expired. You've really got us in a fix now, Fred. You quit on the boss, and you're babbling that me and Curly's gotta do the opposite of what the man who's still our boss wants. We had enough trouble with those two before you started having visions. What'd you have to start hallucinating for?"

"Sh!" Curly exclaimed. "They're listening to ya!"

All three glanced at the ceiling in consternation.

"Oh, fiddle." Chili snatched his covers to his chin. "So what you're telling us is that according to your fevered delusion, we now gotta contrive to keep Michael and Bailey apart?"

"Yep. Unless she makes an honest man out of him in a church."

Chili glanced up warily. "Until *she* makes *him* honest? Aren't we supposed to be working on Michael?"

Fred sighed. "We're talking about Bailey here. You heard Michael. She did hasten from his life without so much as a see-ya-bye. Worse, Polly and Elijah say she's fixing to have a life-altering experience. She may love Michael, but she'll never marry him because she believes he's never going to love her."

"What?" Curly and Chili sat straight up.

"Nope," Fred said sadly. "And that's all Bailey ever wanted, was for Michael to love her."

"It ought to be real easy to keep them apart, then," Curly said. "If they neither of them wants the other."

"Exactly why I tendered my sayonara," Fred said simply. "There's nothing left for me to do here, and I've been antsy to feel useful for a long time. Far as I can see, you can't drag two stubborn mules to the hitch without beating yourself nearly to death in the process." He took a deep breath. "I'm going to work for Gunner King."

Chapter Nine

Michael wasn't certain exactly when his life went askew. Fred had gone over to the enemy, Bailey was on the enemy's payroll, and his mother was in residence. Those things added up to trouble. Nothing was going right. All he knew was that one day he'd been going along peacefully minding his own business, working his ranch and sleeping with the woman he greatly desired every once in a while.

The peace in his life was long departed, and he couldn't quite see what he'd done to bring the disaster he was suffering upon himself.

He sat on his horse staring at the three-way watering hole. Gunner, Bailey and Michael. All three of them bound together by need. "There's one too many of us," he muttered.

Plan A and Plan B had failed miserably. He didn't have a Plan C, and if the ranch hands had one, they weren't telling him. He'd be afraid of any further plans, anyway. They'd landed him in enough of a dilemma.

There had to be a way to get Bailey back on his side of the fence where she belonged. But nobody told Bailey anything. He supposed he could casually mention how it nagged his gut that she was alone in the King mansion every day where Gunner could get his hands on her. Damn, he hated to think about Gunner touching anything of his.

Therein lay the knot. Bailey wasn't his. He'd thought she was, but then she'd showed him how wrong his thinking was. He knew she would refuse an offer of employment from him if he asked her. She'd say that wasn't fair to Gunner.

"Maybe I should just ask her why she quit coming over," he said thoughtfully, his breath white in the freezing air. She'd made her point. After all, she was in his house and could walk up the stairs any time she chose to. But she hadn't chosen to do so, and that was an obvious pointer that something had happened.

Michael chewed both sides of the inside of his suddenly dry mouth. Maybe the answer was as simple as that she just didn't want to make love with him anymore.

That would be the worst thing that ever happened to him. He wanted to make love with her *real* bad. And real often, too.

As much as it was going to upset him to melt his iron control, he had no choice. He would set everything straight and just ask the contrary woman why she'd suddenly vacated his bed during the coldest winter on record in Fallen, Texas.

TO MICHAEL'S DISMAY, his mother was in the kitchen when he entered. "'Morning."

She didn't appear put off by his short greeting. "Good morning." A big smile lit her face. "Have a cup of hot coffee."

"Thanks." He grudgingly took the mug she offered.

"So," she said brightly. "Do you have big plans for tonight?"

He had a plan, but he wasn't going to discuss it with her. "Nope." Saturday night was just the same as any other. He didn't carouse any night of the week.

"Nothing?"

The disappointment in his mother's tone irritated him. "Do you need the house to yourself for some reason? Should I make plans?"

Her face fell. "I just thought perhaps you might be taking Bailey out."

He frowned. "Why would I do that?" He never had before. That wasn't part of their setup.

"I don't know. I thought maybe she seemed a little sweet on you."

Shaking his head, he said, "No." If she was, she wouldn't have left him, but he wasn't going to tell his mother that.

"Oh." Clearly she was dismayed. "I rather thought…well, never mind."

"You rather thought what?" He gave her a suspicious stare.

"Well, with it being Valentine's Day and all, I thought maybe…" Her voice drifted away.

"Is it Valentine's Day?" He glanced at the calendar on the wall, which looked like target practice for all the dates he had circled for this delivery and that pickup, vaccination schedules, et cetera.

Someone had placed a big red sticker heart right smack on the date where only a blind person could miss it. "Very funny, Mother."

"I didn't do it!" She got up to put her plate and mug in the sink. "I just thought there might be a reason for it to be there. Obviously, I was wrong." Shrugging, she pulled on her coat. "Brad's in the throes of artistic fervor, so I was going to offer to watch the children if you were taking Bailey out, but since I'm not needed—"

"Wait." He held up a hand to forestall her exit. "I mean, please hold on a second. I hadn't thought of it, quite frankly." He met her gaze with great discomfort. "We've never, uh, dated before."

"Oh." She nodded, but he read surprise in her careful expression.

Baby ran in the kitchen, her lamb scurrying behind her. They wore matching red ribbons, Baby's in her hair and the lamb's around its neck. "Mr. Michael, happy Valentine's Day!"

She handed him a glue-gooey piece of red paper, which had been cut to resemble a heart with uneven white paper edging.

His own heart began beating uncomfortably. "Uh, thank you, Baby. I'm afraid I don't have anything for you." Or any of the other children. Or his mother. Or Bailey. He felt like a bad guy in a bad western, but Baby beamed at him.

"That's okay. Bailey said you wouldn't. And that I was to tell you it was okay. She said you probably didn't know it was Valentine's Day, 'cause you're not...not, um, man—"

"Romantic?" Cora supplied.

"Yeah!" Baby jumped happily, glue and red marker and glitter on her blue jean overalls. "I put a sticker on your calendar so you'd know it was today, though. Guess you didn't see it."

"Thank you," he murmured. He tucked her valentine in his shirt pocket. "Right next to my heart."

She giggled and squeezed his leg with her little thin

arms before running from the room, her lamb skitter-
ing to keep up.

His mother turned toward the door. He cleared his
throat. "I may take you up on your offer, if Bailey's
schedule is clear tonight."

"If you ask her right, I'm sure she can find some
time." She went out the door without looking back.

Ask her right. He glanced at the sticker, then tapped
the soggy valentine in his shirt pocket. Valentine's
Day. He hadn't paid any attention to the holiday since
grade school. Sighing heavily, he stared at his work-
rough hands. He was a rancher, not a romancer. Bailey
had quit him, and he didn't think it was over flowers.
Since she was working at Gunner's, there was no easy
way to get to her and ask her out for tonight. Well,
easy enough, just a small drive away, but he wasn't
about to expose his pride to Gunner King.

"I could do romantic," he said to no one. It just
hadn't seemed like something Bailey wanted. Oh, a
girl like Deenie would want diamonds and heart-
shaped... Oh, hell. "Underthingies from Dallas," he
said with a groan. He'd seen those in a catalog he'd
caught the hands reading once. They'd barely paid attention to his scoffing.

Maybe he should have been paying closer attention.

But he'd never thought of Bailey in the context of
heart-shaped underthings. She wore cotton panties,
which slid so smoothly down her legs that he always
had an immediate reaction before he even got them
over her toes. He'd found her more than desirable in
her natural state. And theirs hadn't been a meeting of
verbal communication. Again, there might have been
womanly clues he'd missed.

A gut-tightening sight suddenly wrenched his eyes

wide open in disbelief. Through the doorway that connected the dining room to the foyer, sunlight streamed through the windowpanes, illuminating valentine-pink petals. In disbelief, he walked through, carefully stepping on Brad's paint cloth and around the enormous canvas, drawn toward those pink petals. On the antique pie table a tall vase glimmered, showing off the long-stemmed flowers. *Bailey* was written on the florist's card.

Michael's heart sank. The card wasn't opened. He swallowed. A bad feeling stole through him—he hated to think of who might have sent them. Bailey might not ever tell him who the six lovely flowers were from.

It was none of his business, he reminded himself. He turned to go—but was instantly arrested by the enormous bouquet of delicate salmon-colored roses adorning the mahogany sideboard. Tearing into the dining room, his heart thundered as he read the card. *Bailey.* This envelope was still sealed as well. He whirled, his gaze scanning. One more arrangement, this one smaller but filled with fragrantly feminine white and red carnations in a round glass vase, sat on a lace doily atop a north-facing window ledge. He nearly hurdled Brad's paints to read the card. *Bailey.*

A disturbance unlike any he had ever experienced spread through him. Apparently, Bailey had many admirers. If he didn't want to get left out in the cold, he'd best apply himself to a little romancing.

For that, he could use some assistance. He strode up the stairs, where he found the five youngest Dixon children happily exploring their collective creative genius with a package of red construction paper, several leaking glue bottles and uncapped markers haphazardly lying about Bailey's bedroom. They had cut heart chains and twined them over their sister's head-board. School pictures of the children in uneven hearts graced her mirror.

Michael took a deep breath. No doubt his patience would be sorely tried, but he needed help.

"Who wants to help me pick out the right valentine for Bailey?" he asked.

Five children and a lamb jumped to their feet. "You can all come, but the lamb has to stay here," he said warily. To sweeten the pot, he added, "We'll pick up something special for your dinner and bring it back after we get the valentine. Since I forgot it was a special day."

"Strawberry ice cream and pound cake!" the children shouted.

"Ugh. I mean, ah, is that traditional dinner?" Did Bailey allow them to eat dessert for dinner?

"It's what we always have after dinner on Valentine's Day. When we're in our own house. Bailey said she was too busy to make it this year."

Five pairs of eyes looked at him hopefully. He knew he was being worked on, and it felt great to submit to the hero treatment. "We better pick some up, then. Store-bought, but still good, I'm sure."

"Hurray!" They rewarded him with huge smiles.

He just wished he knew how to make Bailey happy as easily.

BAILEY FINISHED UP the last-minute paperwork Gunner had asked her to oversee. She'd been a bit suspicious when he'd asked her to come over on Valentine's Day—a Saturday—to work. But she hadn't seen him, and the work was clearly pressing. She was so relieved. Ever since he had offered to marry her, Bailey had worried that he'd bring the subject up again. But Gunner had been a true gentleman and rarely came to the house while she was working. When he did, they barely exchanged hellos.

She put on her worn gray coat, which was long enough to keep her legs warm, and hurried out to her truck. Though she hadn't had time to bake the children their special Valentine's treat, she was determined to spend the rest of the afternoon alone with them. No doubt this first Valentine's without their parents would be difficult. The children had handled so much already—why did she feel like she'd never be able to fill her parents' shoes? As she passed the roofless family home, Bailey wanted to cry. Nothing was going right. They weren't just going to be roofless soon; they were going to be homeless. Unless Brad's art show went very well, there was no hope of paying the estate taxes. She didn't know what she'd do with the children then. The only thing she could think of was to move to Dallas, into an apartment. But that would take them away from the town and the people they knew, and the friends they played with. It was the last constant they'd had in their lives. She would do whatever she could not to tear this last touchstone from them.

Adding a new baby to the problem hadn't exactly helped.

Brushing aside her worry and pasting a happy smile on her face for the children, Bailey parked the truck and hurried inside. She flew up the stairs. "Brad?"

The children were gone, and so was Brad. She smiled at the paper chains across her headboard. Her siblings were getting better at them every year. Wistfully, she touched the hearts, and the heart-shaped paper frames with each child's photo inside. Her own heart felt achy and pained. They were such good children. They deserved happiness. Was it so much to ask that they keep the only home they'd ever known?

She wanted to cry, but her eyes felt empty, like she'd cried so much lately there were no tears left in her. The phone rang, so she hurried downstairs. Maybe it was Brad, telling her where he'd taken the kids.

It was Brad; she could hear his voice coming over the recorder. She snatched up the phone. "Brad, I'm here."

"Okay. I just wanted to tell you that Doc Watson called the house looking for you."

She frowned. "Why?"

"He didn't say. He just said he needed you to call him back."

"Okay. Where are you?"

"I'm in Fallen, setting up for the showing at Mr. Day's store."

She smiled at the excitement in his voice. "I'll come get the kids out from under your feet." Five little Dixons trying to help would be disastrous to Brad's concentration.

"They're not with me. They went with Michael."

"What?" She could envision the bristly wariness Michael would have etched in his face confronted with all the littlest Dixons. "Where?"

"I don't know. I was getting ready to leave the house when he came and asked if he could take them for a ride. They seemed real anxious to go with him, and quite frankly, I was glad to be able to get down here without them."

"Of course you were," she murmured, feeling a fast surge of guilt because he'd had to wait for her to get off work, and she'd taken longer to finish up. "I'm sorry, Brad. I should have gotten home sooner."

"It's fine. Michael really seemed to want them, so I left right when I'd planned to."

"Okay." She couldn't reconcile Michael wanting her siblings. Shaking her head, she said, "Thanks for calling."

"Don't forget to call Doc Watson."

"Oh. Okay." She was so unnerved she nearly had.

"I'll be home in an hour or so if you can think of something we could do with the kids. They spent all morning making valentines for us."

"I know." She felt more guilt. There had been no time for her to even think of treats, and certainly no money. "I'll think of something. Thanks, Brad." Hanging up the phone, Bailey sighed. She couldn't let them down. They were so good, rarely complaining about missing their folks, always trying to take care of her and Brad. The tears pressed again, harder, urgent, as if she really could cry now. But Doc Watson would hear her strain and start worrying.

Sighing, she took a couple of deep breaths to steady herself before dialing his number. His wife answered, and they exchanged a moment's pleasantries. Bailey closed her eyes, appreciating so much the closeness of a small town and a doctor who cared enough to check on her on a Saturday, a holiday of romantic notions.

"Hello, Bailey!"

The cheer in his voice was heartwarming. "Hi, Dr. Watson. Brad said you called."

"I did. I've got a heck of a valentine for you."

She smiled. "You do?"

"Yes, I do, young lady. I suspected something this week when we did your sonogram, but I wanted to get the other tests back to be conclusive. Happy Valentine's, little mama, you're having twins!''

Bailey's mouth fell open.

''Two sweet cherubs! How's that for something special on Valentine's Day?''

''Um, it's…certainly a surprise. Thank you, Dr. Watson,'' she mumbled, swiftly hanging up the phone before he could hear her distress. Flying upstairs, she threw herself onto the paper-heart-decorated bed to lay in a shocked stupor.

Twins! She was in trouble, times two.

Chapter Ten

Suddenly, Bailey heard the thunder of Dixon feet, and Michael's deep voice downstairs. She jumped up, rushed into the bathroom and splashed cold water on her face. She was red and blotchy, but there was no help for it. The children might not notice.

Michael certainly would, unless she could avoid him.

When she emerged, five small Dixons, one small lamb and one big, strong and fiercely handsome male grinned hugely at her. "Surprise!" they exclaimed.

She met Michael's gaze, startled. "What have you been doing?"

"We got the cake!" Baby cried.

"And the ice cream!" Amy added.

"And—" Sam began.

"Sh!" Michael reminded him. He put on an innocent expression. "We went shopping. The children have been teaching me the proper way to celebrate Valentine's Day. We have some surprises for you."

I have a big one for you, cowboy, she thought. But of course, she couldn't ruin the happiness of the moment. He was so proud, so pleased by what he'd done with the kids. They were all enormously puffed up

with their surprises for her. It would ruin their pleasure
if she didn't go along with their plans. Pulling out her
brightest smile, Bailey made herself be delighted.

She jumped onto her bed, crossed her legs and
closed her eyes. Folding her hands in her lap, she said,
"Okay, I'm ready."

Michael stared at Bailey, who'd suddenly gone yoga
on him. "What's she doing?" he whispered to the
kids.

"Waiting for her surprise," Paul explained.

"Oh." He would never have guessed. "What do
we do now?"

Beth giggled. "We surprise her."

He could think of a surprise he'd like to visit on
her. The way she sat there, all expectantly, her eyes
closed, her lips slightly curved in a waiting smile—it
was all he could do not to plant a big valentine kiss
on her and roll her into the sheets. But this was the
Dixon way, and he was supposed to be learning.
"How do we do that?"

The children all glanced at each other with anticipation. Slowly, Baby went forward, placing a plastic
blue rose in her sister's outstretched hand. She giggled
as she did, then rushed back to her place in the group
without saying anything to Bailey.

Bailey ran exploring fingers over the valentine.
"Not a paper something? Has Michael been assisting
you with your artwork?"

He didn't know what to make of that, but Baby
giggled.

Bailey smiled. "Ah, I heard you, Baby. This is from
you. It's a flower."

"Right!" Baby beamed, and went forward to accept
the kisses her sister rained on her.

"Thank you, Baby." Bailey resumed her position.

Michael waited for the next cue. Beth went forward, placing a small heart-shaped box in Bailey's hand.

"Hmm. Michael *has* been helping you."

"What does that mean, exactly?" he demanded.

"We always make our own valentines," Beth explained.

"Ah. We should have been trickier and only bought paper things." He shot Bailey a disgruntled frown, but she couldn't see him, of course. "You didn't tell me we were deviating from the plan. It gave her the position of power," he complained to the children.

They giggled.

"You didn't let them spend a lot of your money, did you?" Bailey's expression was worried, though her eyes remained closed.

"Every gift was under three dollars," he told her. "Don't spoil this for us."

"Okay." She smiled again. "This is from Beth, because she keeps talking to Michael, so I know it's her turn. And it's a pretty little box, and I love it. Next."

"Greedy, isn't she?" Michael was rewarded by the children's laughter.

One by one, they tried to outwit Bailey, but she always guessed which child, and the gift put in her hand. Finally, it was his turn.

"Don't open your eyes!" Baby told her.

"Why?" Bailey asked.

"Because we're not done," Amy explained.

"It's five valentines." Bailey cocked her head, frowning.

The children pushed Michael forward. He walked lightly, so she wouldn't hear his heavier footsteps, and reaching as far out in front of him as he could, he dropped something into Bailey's hands.

She seemed puzzled as she felt it. "Well…is it from Michael?"

"Yes!" Her siblings laughed, their gazes meeting his with hushed delight.

"If she can't guess what it is, what happens?" he asked them.

"You get the prize," Baby told him, so excited that she was bouncing up and down.

"Which is what?" he wanted to know.

"A kiss," Sam said, matter-of-factly.

"A big kiss, lots of kissies," Amy explained. "And raspberries. Lots of loud wet ones."

"Oh." He raised his brow at them and made a scared face. Bailey was still feeling over the object in her hands with curiosity. "I think I'm too big to be given raspberries."

"You'd like it," Paul told him. "We all pile on. Anyway, Mom gave Dad raspberries all the time."

Bailey raised a brow though her eyes were closed. "I'm not giving you a raspberry, Michael. I'm going to figure out what this is in a second. Under three dollars, small, soft…" She ticked off the list to herself.

The Dixon raspberries had been an endearment rather than an insult. It stung for just a moment that this family enjoyed each other so much. Why had he not had a close relationship with his parents? Why had his family been so distant with each other?

Suddenly, he was looking forward to receiving his kiss and piling on and blowing raspberries. "How many guesses does she get?"

"Only one." Beth grinned. "Give up, Bailey?"

"Never!"

The children giggled. Michael felt himself filling with anticipation. Bailey's lips were bare and naturally pink, and he remembered all too well what they felt like against his.

He couldn't wait.

She turned the object over one last time. "A soft valentine? Like a tiny pillow?"

"We told you," Paul said. "She can figure anything out."

"You can open your eyes and see, Bailey," Baby said.

Bailey did, tracing the glittery lettering that was stitched into the tacky valentine with her finger. "Beautiful Baby, be mine," she read out loud, and then she burst into tears.

"Oh, Bailey!" all the children cried, rushing forward to hug and squeeze their sister and pat her back soothingly. For some reason their concern seemed to make her cry harder.

Where were the kissies, the raspberries and the pile-on? Michael shifted awkwardly from boot to boot. What had happened?

"She's been crying a lot lately," Beth told him in a wise voice. "I think she misses our folks," she whispered.

Bailey clung to the children, who clumped to her like so many pieces of wool. Michael swallowed hard. Maybe she was missing her folks. Maybe the burden of raising this crew was getting to her. He knew the inheritance tax bill was due soon, too—Brad's art show that they hoped would do well was right before they had to pay the money. Michael shook his head, sad for all of them. He felt tears coming to his eyes. It wasn't fair that the children had to be so distressed.

They should still be carefree children, with no worries other than what game they might play today. He didn't want Bailey to cry anymore.

He cleared his throat. ''Maybe you kids could go downstairs and start dishing up the ice cream. Paul, if you can cut carefully, you can put the cake on some plates. I'll bring your sister downstairs in a moment.''

One by one, they kissed their sister before filing silently downstairs. He stared at the golden-haired woman he wanted so much to help. He just didn't have the first clue as to how.

Slowly, he sat next to her. Then he thought better of it and went into the bathroom, snatching up some tissues to push into her hand before sitting again. She blew her nose loudly and he rubbed her back. ''Better?''

She shook her head. ''I feel worse. I ruined the valentine surprise.''

''It's not ruined. I can hear the kids downstairs getting down the bowls and plates, so they're happy again.'' He reached to twine a piece of her hair behind her ear so he could see her face. ''I'd like to know why you didn't like my valentine.''

''Oh, Michael,'' she whispered.

''Yes?''

''I really don't know. I mean, I do like it. I like all of them, and I appreciate you taking them out and helping them with a big surprise. They had so much fun.'' She tried to smile at him through watery eyes. ''I think I just got caught off guard or something.''

He took the pillow she still clutched in one hand. ''To be honest, Baby picked it out. I think her name being on it was a big draw. We thought it would make

PLAY THE
Lucky Key Game
and get

HOW TO PLAY:

1. With a coin, carefully scratch off gold area at the right. Then check the claim chart to see what we have for you — **FREE BOOKS** and a **FREE GIFT** — **ALL YOURS FREE!**

2. Send back this card and you'll receive brand-new Harlequin American Romance® novels. These books have a cover price of $3.99 each in the U.S. and $4.50 each in Canada, but they are yours to keep absolutely free.

3. There's no catch. You're under no obligation to buy anything. We charge nothing — ZERO — for your first shipment. And you don't have to make any minimum number of purchases — not even one!

4. The fact is thousands of readers enjoy receiving books by mail from the Harlequin Reader Service® months before they're available in stores. They like the convenience of home delivery and they love our discount prices!

5. We hope that after receiving your free books you'll want to remain a subscriber. But the choice is yours — to continue or cancel, any time at all! So why not take us up on our invitation, with no risk of any kind. You'll be glad you did!

YOURS FREE!
A SURPRISE MYSTERY GIFT

We can't tell you what it is...but we're sure you'll like it! A
FREE GIFT—
just for playing the LUCKY KEY game!

FREE GIFTS!

NO COST! NO OBLIGATION TO BUY!
NO PURCHASE NECESSARY!

PLAY THE
Lucky Key Game

Scratch gold area with a coin.
Then check below to see the gifts you get!

YES! I have scratched off the gold area. Please send me the 2 Free books and gift for which I qualify. I understand I am under no obligation to purchase any books, as explained on the back and on the opposite page.

354 HDL CX9Z   **154 HDL CX9P**

Name
_____
(PLEASE PRINT CLEARLY)

Address _____ Apt.#

                                                            Postal
City _____ State/Prov. _____ Zip/Code

2 free books plus a mystery gift	1 free book
2 free books	Try Again!

Offer limited to one per household and not valid to current Harlequin American Romance® subscribers. All orders subject to approval.

(H-AR-02/00)
PRINTED IN U.S.A.

The Harlequin Reader Service® — Here's how it works:

Accepting your 2 free books and gift places you under no obligation to buy anything. You may keep the books and gift and return the shipping statement marked "cancel." If you do not cancel, about a month later we'll send you 4 additional novels and bill you just $3.34 each in the U.S., or $3.71 each in Canada, plus 25¢ delivery per book and applicable taxes if any.* That's the complete price and — compared to cover prices of $3.99 each in the U.S. and $4.50 each in Canada — it's quite a bargain! You may cancel at any time, but if you choose to continue, every month we'll send you 4 more books, which you may either purchase at the discount price or return to us and cancel your subscription.

*Terms and prices subject to change without notice. Sales tax applicable in N.Y. Canadian residents will be charged applicable provincial taxes and GST.

If offer card is missing write to: Harlequin Reader Service, 3010 Walden Ave., P.O. Box 1867, Buffalo NY 14240-1867

BUSINESS REPLY MAIL
FIRST-CLASS MAIL   PERMIT NO. 717   BUFFALO, NY

POSTAGE WILL BE PAID BY ADDRESSEE

HARLEQUIN READER SERVICE
3010 WALDEN AVE
PO BOX 1867
BUFFALO NY 14240-9952

NO POSTAGE
NECESSARY
IF MAILED
IN THE
UNITED STATES

you laugh." He grimaced at her. "I wish you wouldn't cry, Bailey. It scares me when you do."

She wiped her eyes. "Why?"

Shrugging, he said, "Because I don't know how to help you. I don't feel like things are the same...I don't know what you need. Or what you want."

She gazed at him with soft, wondering eyes. "I don't know what you want, either."

"I want you to be happy. I know it's hard on you right now." He scratched his cheek thoughtfully before taking a deep breath. "Bailey, look. Your parents had no life insurance?"

She slowly shook her head.

"At the risk of upsetting you, I have a suggestion. Not even a suggestion, more like a request."

The tissue was balled up in the sudden fist she made. "What?"

Reaching over to rub the fist so she'd relax her hand but mainly so he could feel her, he said, "Bailey, I'd like to pay the inheritance taxes on your property."

She stiffened. "No, thank you. I mean, thank you, but no."

He frowned. "Can you tell me why? You say no that quickly—" he snapped his fingers "—without even thinking over my offer."

"No, Michael. I don't know any other answer except that."

"Bailey, the children said you cry all the time. I can take the financial stress from you, and then you can go back to being the Bailey they need right now. They don't have much except you and Brad, and they should have the you they still want! The one who blows raspberries and dispenses kissies and smiles."

Bailey looked away from him. He gently turned her

chin toward him. "I'd like the old you back, myself," he said huskily.

She took a deep breath. "It's not that easy anymore."

"Let me make it easier."

Silence enveloped the room. Bailey removed his hand from her chin and set it on his leg before scooting an inch further away from him on the bed. The last rays of chill gray afternoon shrouded the room.

"Come eat!" Paul hollered up the stairs.

"It's not the way I want it," she finally said to Michael as she stood. "I don't want you making things easier for me. I know you could, but it wasn't why I was coming around."

"I know that! What do you think, if I help you with the taxes, it's like paying you for...sex? Bailey, maybe a quarter of the farmers and ranchers I know are trying to figure out how to get Uncle Sam and his damn tax bills off their backs right now. They may end up losing everything they've struggled for years to build. You're just one woman, with a huge family." He put his hands on her shoulders earnestly. "You can accept a little help and not feel like it's charity."

"Not from you."

Leaning back so he could look into her eyes, he frowned. "What's that mean? That you could from Gunner? He thinks up a job for you, and you go over to his house every day so he's got the chance to hit on you? He pays you for that, but you can accept his so-called help?"

"Gunner doesn't hit on me," she said tightly.

"Oh, sure. Then what do you call all those flower arrangements downstairs?"

She raised her brows. "What flower arrangements?"

"You didn't see that the dining room has been turned into a florist shop?"

"No. I didn't." She pulled away from him. "I don't understand you. You say you want to help me, but...but—"

"But what?" If she'd just tell him, he'd do anything he could. "What would help you, Bailey?"

Her teeth chewed deep into her bottom lip before she answered. "All I ever wanted was for you to love me, Michael."

He stepped back a pace, his emotions in a tight, astonished vise. She shrugged at him but didn't say another word.

"Ice cream's melting!" Baby shouted up the stairs.

He didn't know what to say. Love? Did she love him? Did they love each other? Never having given deep thought to that area of his heart, he veered away from it now. He liked her. He'd enjoyed her living in his house more than he'd thought he would. They didn't bicker and suffer long, angry silences the way his parents had.

But did that mean he loved her?

"What if I say okay, maybe I love you?" he asked. "Then what?"

She hesitated, her heart hovering painfully inside her. "I really don't know. I suppose it's up to you."

He needed more information than that. "And what if I say that I don't love you? That I like you, but that's all I can feel?"

"Then I suppose I'll have to say the same thing I said to your other offer. No, thanks."

He frowned. "What are we talking about here, exactly? Because I'm just a little confused. You're wanting something from me, some right answer, but I've got a dining room full of flowers, which would give me the idea that I'm not the only man in the picture, and—''

''Let me go see these flowers that have you so confused.'' She hurried down the stairs. He followed closely behind.

''Oh, my goodness,'' he heard her say. Yeah. Oh, my goodness. That was exactly what he'd thought. He watched as she picked up the card in front of the six valentine-pink roses in the tall, elegant vase.

''They're so pretty,'' she murmured.

''Lovely.''

She sent him a sharp look and opened the card. ''Thanks for all your help. Gunner.''

''Lovelier still.''

She set the card down slowly. ''You know, I think you're jealous.''

''Oh, no. Not me.'' Palms up, he waved his hands in a negating motion. ''Not of Gunner King, you can bet your last dime on that.''

Instantly, he wished he hadn't mentioned money. Bailey's gaze hardened as she turned away. She slowly picked up the card in front of the salmon-colored roses. ''Happy Valentine's Day to the best li'l gal around. Chili, Curly and Fred.'' Mutinously, she glanced at Michael, but he was feeling so relieved, like a ten-pound weight had dropped off him, that he could only shrug.

''No smart remark?'' she asked.

''Well, Fred's a darn traitor, and the other two are schemers.''

''And you're acting like a selfish child.''

"What? What does that mean?"

"Why haven't you gone over to Gunner's and told Fred you need him at the Walking W?" Hands on her hips, she glared at him.

"He's the one who left."

"Oh, *he's* the one who left. *I'm* the one who wants you to love me, and that's just my tough luck, isn't it? We're all just tough-luck cases, and you don't have any responsibility in the matter."

He didn't like the way she made him sound like a slack. Brad was slack when it came to making decisions. Her father had been useless. But Michael was neither of those, and he didn't want to be lumped in with men who couldn't handle the load. "I'm not going to argue with you," he said stiffly.

"Of course you're not," she snapped, "because that would take some emotion, and though you might spend every penny to ease your conscience and make yourself feel good by taking care of your poor neighbors, you're not about to spend any of that emotion you keep so carefully hoarded away and guarded."

Her voice had risen, and her stance was angry. The moment felt an awful lot like a hundred he'd seen as a child. Michael didn't move.

She sighed, snatching the card in front of the red and white carnations. "Happy Valentine's Day. You were a charming child, but you've turned into a wonderful woman." She glanced at Michael. "Cora Wade."

He was thunderstruck. His mother had sent the flowers?

"Aren't you just a little bit ashamed, Michael? These bouquets are all from people who are trying to make my life a little brighter."

He swallowed. "I *was* jealous."

"I know." She stared at him. "I put a flower vase in the kitchen. It has one rose in it, but that was all I could afford. It's for your mother, and I'd like you to sign the card before she gets home. The least you can do is treat your mother the way she deserves while she's here chaperoning me. Although, Lord knows, the cow is long past the barn door for that."

She swept from the room to join the children in the kitchen. He heard their happy greetings and the laughter. Bailey was right. His mother had been trying, and he'd ignored her efforts. And the cow *was* long past the barn door, because he and Bailey had been intimate. On a sexual level, anyway.

And suddenly he realized that was the problem. He strode into the kitchen. "You're right," he said. He walked over to the bud vase with a white rose in it and signed the card as she'd requested. The children paused in their snacking. Bailey waited.

"I'd like to start over," he told her. "With the barn door closed this time. So I can…work at this a little harder. See where things end up. Don't get me wrong. I still wish the barn door was wide open. But I think we've got something here, and—" he glanced around at the kids who stared at him "—maybe we should go at it from a, um, new direction. Like dating."

A smile spread over her face. "Really?"

"I think so."

"Aren't you going to have any ice cream and cake?" Baby asked.

He took the chair next to her. "I think I will." He was awfully glad to be included in their family circle.

The back door opened, and his mother walked in. "Oh, a party!"

A cold draft blew in with her. Michael felt the familiar defensive posture he always had with his mother. Bailey's gaze was on him, so he stood. "Join us, Mother."

"All right. I will." Pleased, she seated herself next to Bailey.

"Thank you for the lovely flowers, Cora," Bailey said.

"Oh, you're welcome, dear."

Cora beamed. Bailey passed her some cake and ice cream. Michael drummed his fingers on the table for a second before reaching to snatch the bud vase from the kitchen counter. He put it in front of his mother. Her eyes grew enormous.

"Happy Valentine's Day," he said gruffly.

She bowed her head, but he could see her delighted expression. "Thank you, son," was all she said, but it was enough. By the grateful look in Bailey's eyes, it was better than enough.

And suddenly, he knew, with all the certainty of time that had been in existence before he was born, and would be in existence after he died, that he loved Bailey Dixon with all his heart. No cheap, tacky, funny valentine heart with a cute saying could express it. He loved her deeply. He loved her for forever.

Somehow, the thought was very worrisome. Maybe it meant marriage one day. Marriage. Maybe it meant children of their own. He digested that.

But what other way could it be? He loved that girl, with her long silky hair and the tiny freckles on her nose. He loved her body and he loved her spunk. They had gotten through their first argument without any battle wounds, and that was a good sign, wasn't it?

He saw how Bailey and his mother smiled at each

other warmly, with respect and friendship. His father had never smiled at his mother. There had been no smiles in their home.

His father hadn't been one for laughter. Or affection.

He didn't want to be like his father. As far as he could see, the Wades might have had all the money, but the Dixons had possessed all the love. One of them had died poor but rich in spirit, and the other had died a broken man.

He'd rather be loved by his wife like Mr. Dixon had been than scorned by his wife like his own father.

He'd passed judgment wrongly. It was time to set that right. Old habits would be hard to break, but to keep that smile on Bailey's face, he was going to do his darnedest to change his ways. The cowboys would say an old dog couldn't be taught new tricks.

Plan C—throw away the old plans and quit planning. I can learn a new trick or two, or however many it takes.

Chapter Eleven

Only pride had kept Bailey from accepting Michael's offer to pay the inheritance taxes. She wanted him to love her and the babies they were going to have. Maybe it was silly to so desperately want him to say he loved her. For her, marriage was only good between two people who respected each other, and she wanted to start off this new phase of their relationship with Michael's full respect. She didn't know if he had marriage in mind, but if he did, it had to be because he loved her—not just because they were having babies.

She frowned as she put the dishes away. There hadn't been a good time to tell him about the additional bundle of joy. Twins! She still hadn't quite gotten over the shock of that. Two names, two of everything—the thought was boggling.

She smiled, thinking Michael was going to be very surprised when he found out. He'd been very busy in the week after Valentine's, and they hadn't seen each other much. Chili and Curly were slow-going on her roof without Fred, but Brad was painting up a storm. He wouldn't let anyone see his masterpiece. He'd even cordoned off the room so the children couldn't run through and upset his work area.

She worried about Brad. What if no one came to the showing today? Mr. Day seemed extremely confident. He'd advertised the event in neighboring towns and touted an auction for the huge canvas Brad had put the final touches on last week. A truck had pulled up to the house, courtesy of Mr. Day, and movers had carefully wrapped the painting and carried it into town.

Poor Brad. He wanted any money he received from the showing to go toward paying the inheritance tax, but she was so afraid he might be disappointed. Crushed. He was a sensitive brother, kind and gentle. But the term "starving artist" was in existence for a reason. There was no reason to heap great expectations on a day in a small town where there were probably few art connoisseurs.

Bailey shook her head, wishing she knew the end to all the works in progress around her—her roof, Brad's showing, the twins she had yet to bond to and Michael, the biggest work in progress of all. Since they'd agreed to start over, he had barely come near her. He was polite in the mornings when he saw her, remote as a television reporter speaking about mundane things. He smiled, but stiffly, when he returned at night.

Bailey dried her hands and took off the apron. It was time to get the children ready to head into town. She had such nerves she wasn't sure she could enjoy herself. No doubt Michael was too busy to attend, and maybe that was a good thing. If anything, their comfort level around each other had decreased, which made her sad.

The taxes would not be met by Brad's showing. No matter how much folks were trying to help, it was an impossibly large sum.

Knowing that, and the reality that there would be not one but two extra mouths to feed, Bailey had done the only thing she could so that their family wouldn't live on well-meaning charity. That was what even kind Mr. Day was trying to do—figure out a way to get money to the Dixons without injuring their pride. But the Dixons were sitting on a resource of their own, and she had decided to sell it.

Gunner King had offered to pay a fair market price for the land and the watering hole. The Dixons would keep their house and the small front yard. She and Brad had discussed it, and he'd agreed, though he hoped for great things from his showing. He was a dreamer, and she understood that. But they needed hard cash right now.

Michael's offer to pay off the inheritance taxes had made her realize she could no longer put off the inevitable. The Dixons might be poor, but they still had pride. After Michael's offer, she knew she couldn't offer the land to him. He would leap on the chance to give her all the money she needed.

But she wanted his love. She would settle for nothing else.

"Bailey!" Michael called from upstairs.

She went to the staircase and looked up. "Yes?"

"Do you want to ride into Fallen with me? You and the kids?"

"You're going to the showing?"

He was madly whisking a razor over his face. "I wouldn't miss Brad's big success for anything."

"I hope it is a success." She couldn't help worrying.

"Did you see the masterpiece?" He stopped shaving for a moment.

"No."

"Well, I did." He grinned. "I sneaked a glance when Brad wasn't looking, before they hauled it off. There's going to be some fireworks in town."

That didn't sound good. "Wasn't it a good painting?"

He shrugged. "I thought it was great. So, are you going to ride with me or not? I mean, Bailey, may I take you into town today?"

"Oh, stop," she said, starting to smile. "You're making me crazy with all this formality. Starting over didn't mean completely from scratch, did it?"

"I guess it doesn't have to."

He stared down the stairs at her, and she just stood there, admiring the way he looked in blue jeans and a flannel shirt. His hair lay damply on his collar, his face was half-shaven, but he looked so handsome her heart beat crazily. "Maybe you could fast-forward the process just a little."

"Miss me, do you?" He raised his brows suggestively.

"Yes, but not enough to give up on our decision to get to know each other outside of...you know." She couldn't say "the bedroom" in case the children overheard. "I thought it was a much better idea than your other one."

"Just checking. Hey, what other one?"

"When you had my roof removed." She smiled at him, her expression teasing. "Honestly, Michael, you could have saved yourself a lot of trouble if you'd just said you wanted to see me more often."

"Well, I've got to work up to these things."

"So how's it going?"

"The roof? It should be done today. When you get

home from the showing, I expect to see a roof that even the most persistent Texas thunderstorm can't leak through. And no roof worms, either.''

Her heart sank. "Today?"

"That's what the roofing company I hired assured me.''

"I...see." For some reason, it wasn't welcome news. When she'd asked how it was going, she'd meant the exploring of their relationship. She hadn't been thinking about returning to her own house. Obviously, Michael had.

Somehow, that knowledge relieved her mind all over again about selling her property to Gunner. She wouldn't be able to bear hearing Michael swiftly agree to buy her land—and never so willingly want *her*.

DEENIE WAS READY for her big day. Brad had promised her the painting was huge and eye-popping, the best thing he'd ever done. She felt all shivery just thinking about the auction her daddy had decided to hold for the one prize canvas, the queen of the showing. All Brad's other paintings would be on display for sale, but hers, the one of her in her sparkling long blue evening gown and elegant, expensive beaded shoes, her hair coiffed elaborately, that one was the jewel. She wished Brad had let her see it, but he said it was bad luck, or that it would hinder his artistic muse, or some artistic reasoning like that, which was utter silliness. She hadn't pressed him about seeing it, though maybe she should have insisted on giving him her opinion of his work. He'd worked from a photograph of her, one taken quite a while ago, of course. Long past her triumphant rodeo queen years, it had been a while since she'd worn a crown of any kind.

She'd given the picture to him so he'd know exactly how she wanted to be commemorated on canvas.

She shivered again, the anticipation thrilling her. *Maybe Daddy will see that my portrait brings in so much money that he can't possibly cut off my allowance!* She was Deenie Day, an acknowledged beauty throughout Texas, just like Scarlett O'Hara in her glory days. A delicate and exotic rose, she deserved pampering.

Smiling into the mirror, she sprayed her hair one more time—in case a Texas-size wind decided to blow—put on a little more shiny lipstick in case anybody took her picture and then curtsied to an imaginary court of admirers.

Perfect. Her new life as someone famous, maybe a model or movie star, was beginning. Fallen would talk about Deenie Day and how they'd known her when, but she planned to be long gone from here.

The only thing bothering her about that scenario was Brad. She hated to admit it, but she thought about the artist all the time. His kiss stayed in her mind, playing over and over, like a tune she couldn't learn the words to. It was disturbing. She hated thinking about him!

And yet, when he'd held her in his arms, she'd felt strangely comfortable. Accepted, somehow, for herself. Just Deenie Day, not the Rodeo Queen, but Deenie, with all her faults unquestioned.

She'd be the laughingstock of Fallen if she allowed herself to fall in love with a Dixon. Everyone expected her to make the most advantageous and socially brilliant match Fallen had ever seen.

But she couldn't wait to see how he'd captured her beauty on canvas. Her daddy said Brad was a rare treasure, a once-in-a-century artist he was privileged to discover. Deenie had never heard her daddy talk like that before. Shivers ran along her arms again.

It was going to be the most glorious day of her life.

"ARE YOU GOING to the big shindig in town?" Chili shouted at Fred, who was perched all alone on the fence sectioning Bailey's and Gunner's properties. Chili and Curly were atop the cross-timber fence that divided Bailey's and Michael's properties. Chili was worried about his friend. Fred never visited the Walking W anymore.

"Yeah, I'm going," Fred called across Bailey's narrow front yard. "You?"

"Wouldn't miss it. We're gonna drag Mrs. Wade along with us. Thought she might enjoy a day off her chaperoning."

They all glanced to Bailey's roof, which the crew was swiftly finishing.

"'Pears she won't be needed much longer," Fred called.

"You could be right. Hey, why don't you come over here so we don't have to keep shouting?" Chili hollered.

Fred shook his head. "I don't sit on no fence whereupon I'm not employed."

Chili and Curly glanced at each other. Sighing, Chili hopped down. Curly did, too, and they went and joined Fred on the King fence. "Anybody ever tell you you're a stubborn cuss?"

"Yep." Fred nodded. "But a man's gotta do what's right."

"If you're waiting for Michael to come get you, you've got a long wait ahead of you."

Fred shrugged. "I ain't going back. He's not doing right by Bailey, and I made a deathbed promise to her folks. I intend to keep that promise."

"I do not understand why you think your absence is going to help those two get together, but then I rarely did understand you," Curly complained.

"Michael's gonna have to learn to think for himself," Fred stated. "He's so much like his pa I don't even know if he can be anything else but mulish."

"He gave Cora a rose for Valentine's. That's progress, ain't it?" Chili wanted to know.

"Bailey bought that. I seen her in town."

"Oh." Chili thought that over. "He took that passel of kids and let them buy little surprises for their sister."

"He shoulda bought Bailey an engagement ring," Fred asserted.

Curly and Chili shook their heads.

"I mean, what was he thinking?" Fred fumed. "It's too bad he's got no father to guide him in these matters, not that Michael Senior would've been much help."

"Nope," Curly and Chili agreed.

"So I'm going into town 'cause I ain't got nothing better to do." Fred sighed. "It's a pretty day, and I'm hoping Brad makes a ton of green on his paintings because Bailey's selling her land to Gunner."

"What?" Chili nearly toppled off the fence.

"You heard me," Fred said grimly. "I'm serving as a double agent at this point. I know what's going on both here and there, and I say things are about to get out of hand. 'Cause you can bet your dirty, worn-out boots that as soon as Michael finds out what she's done, there's going to be some serious turmoil."

"I hope the rivalry doesn't flare up again," Curly said worriedly. "Elijah's not here to throw water on their hot heads."

"Come on," Fred said, getting down from the fence. "Let's get Mrs. Wade and scoot into town. If we have to pull folks in off the street to buy Brad's work, then that's what we'll do."

"Great. Now we're street peddlers," Chili griped.

"I'd rather be that than peacekeepers trying to douse young-buck tempers," Fred asserted. "I do wish Bailey hadn't gone and done that. Gunner was so happy I know he's just itching to rub it in Michael's face. He's got no water allowance now for his cattle."

"Come on, Curly," Chili said through clenched teeth. "Let's get Cora and go!"

MICHAEL HELPED Bailey and her noisy crew into his car. "You look mighty pretty," he told her as he got in.

"What about me?" Baby wanted to know from her place between them.

"You look like a princess. I've got a carload of handsome gents and beautiful young ladies."

By the giggles in the back seat, he decided that had met with everyone's approval. Bailey only offered a terse smile.

"Something wrong?" he asked.

She barely shook her head. "I've got nerves."

He reached over Baby to pat Bailey's leg. "I think I do, too."

"Why?"

Pulling the car down the drive, he shrugged. "I don't know. Just want Brad's day to go well, I guess."

"You just want his paints and canvases out of your dining room," Bailey teased.

He grinned. "I don't use that room, so I've hardly noticed him being around except for a whiff of paint occasionally." Bailey smiled, so he hoped he was making her feel better. It would be nerve-racking to have work on display for the first time. He did want everything to go well for Brad.

Brad and Bailey and the children and the lamb would go back to their house tonight. That would leave him alone with his mother, a thought that was distinctly unsettling. He wondered if he'd ever feel truly comfortable around her. As far as he was concerned, she *had* deserted him. His father had been a difficult man—there was no denying that. But the pain of his parents' separation had cut through his adolescence with a wide, uncaring knife. He rarely dated. He didn't make a lot of friends.

Until Bailey slipped so easily into his life he hardly noticed she'd entered a place he never allowed anyone—his heart.

He understood her nerves. He had plenty of them right now himself.

"Oh, my gosh, would you look at all the people?" Bailey exclaimed.

Families milled around Day's House of Fine Art and Jewelry, spilling out onto the sidewalks, where painting after painting was on display.

"Are those all Brad's?" Michael asked.

"I suppose so."

Bailey voice was tight. Michael heard the edginess. He reached over to gently tug her hair. "It's going to be fine."

"I sure hope so."

"Brad's going to be famous!" Paul said in awe. "Some people have already bought paintings!"

Indeed, there were workers carefully wrapping and binding canvases to be carried to cars.

"It looks like all of Dallas is here," Michael murmured.

"I'm so scared," Bailey said under her breath. "I've got to find Brad."

"I'm sure he's fine. What time is the unveiling of the masterpiece?"

"At two."

So in ten minutes the auction would begin. Michael grinned. "Look, there goes Deenie."

The Rodeo Queen rode past in an open convertible. Streamers blew from the antenna, and a sign on the side of the car proclaimed *Come bid on the one-of-a-kind painting everybody's talking about!* Deenie waved at the crowd and tossed candy.

"She's in her element," Bailey muttered.

"If it brings Brad business, we can stand a little of her show ponying. Come on." Michael helped the children out of the car, and then Bailey. Her face was white and worried.

"Do you feel all right?" he asked, glancing at the sky. The weather was perfect, with a tepid breeze blowing just enough to keep the crowd in a good, comfortable mood. But maybe Bailey was too hot standing in the sun. "Why don't we walk under the awnings?"

"I'm fine."

Her thin smile said she was not. "Hey," he said suddenly. "Beth, as the oldest, you're in charge. See that cotton candy and ice cream vendor over there? You and Paul take your siblings' hands and carefully cross over and get one goody for everyone. Here's some money, Beth. Uh-uh,'' he reprimanded Bailey, when she tried to protest, ''my treat.''

''All right.'' She subsided hesitantly. ''Thank you.''

The kids ran off, not heeding his instructions about being careful at all. Fortunately, the street in front of the Day store was so crammed with pedestrians that cars—other than Deenie's convertible—were taking alternate routes. ''Do you want something?''

She shook her head.

''It's going to be fine,'' he told her, pulling her arm through his. ''Nothing could possibly spoil this wonderful day.'' He looked around, spying Brad near the stage. ''There's your brother. The kids can still see us, so let's go congratulate him.'' He took Bailey's arm and steered her toward the stage.

''Bailey!'' Brad exclaimed, clearly relieved to see her. ''A friendly face. Yours, too, Michael.''

''I'm so proud of you!'' She hugged Brad fiercely. ''I've been so worried that it wouldn't go well, but look at all the people!''

He managed a wry chuckle. ''I never dreamed there'd be this kind of a crowd. And they're actually buying!'' Glancing around to make certain only she and Michael could hear his next words, he said, ''I think we're going to have a little more to pay on the taxes than we ever dreamed!''

''Oh, Brad. We don't have to worry anymore. Please don't think about that on your special day. I took care of it.''

Michael saw Brad's attention focus sharply on his sister. ''You did?''

She nodded. Michael perked up. How in heck could she have taken care of that whopping bill?

"I did," she confirmed. "I'm positive we made the right decision."

Brad glanced at Michael cautiously, but Michael pretended he hadn't noticed. This was a personal moment that didn't concern him. He felt guilty listening in when he should be selecting a painting of Brad's to help out the Dixon family cause. Buying a painting wouldn't injure Bailey's pride. He began to eye the canvases lining the sidewalk behind Brad. The children joined them, their hands full of snow cones and other frozen snacks. "How can you eat that in the dead of winter?"

Baby grinned, her lips purple with grape syrup. "It's 'licious!"

"Are you going to thank Mr. Wade?" Bailey demanded.

"Thank you, Mr. Wade!" the children chorused.

Somebody clapped him on the back, and he turned to see his two cowboys, one deserter and his mother, who could also be classified as a deserter. "Howdy, everyone," he said mildly.

"Quite a gathering you got here, Brad," Chili said congenially. "Reckon you're gonna be famous one day."

Brad smiled self-consciously. The artist was real anxious, and Michael could commiserate. He didn't like surprises himself; the unknown was something he took care to avoid. He kept a careful handle on everything he could control. That which he couldn't, like cattle prices, he simply tried to hedge his bets against.

He wouldn't be in Brad's position for anything. How miserable it must be to have his pride on the line in front of a bunch of gawkers!

"Thanks for coming, everyone. It means a lot," Brad said.

"We've got to support the home team," Cora Wade replied.

"That reminds me. I brought you a boutonniere." Bailey reached into her purse and pulled out a single rosebud backed by greenery that looked like it had been fashioned from one of her valentine bouquets. She handed it to Brad, but Deenie had come to stand next to him, and Brad suddenly became even more nervous. He turned, pinning the boutonniere to Deenie's dress.

She smiled, unpinned it and said, "Hold still," to Brad.

He did, like he was stuck to the ground. Michael was amazed to see how he drank in the woman while she carefully attached the rose to the lapel of Brad's suit jacket. If it had been him she was touching, he'd have jumped a country mile to get away from her.

But from the look in Brad's eyes, it was obvious there was no place he'd rather be.

"Thanks, Deenie," he murmured.

"I've got to go," she told him. "Come on. Daddy wants you, too."

Like a sleepwalker, he followed her up the stage steps.

The group glanced around at each other in astonishment.

"Well, I never," Chili said.

"Wow, did you see all the spangles on her dress?" Beth asked. "She looks like a princess!"

"Brad's in luuuv!" Amy cried jubilantly.

"I want to be a princess," Baby stated.

"Oh, but you are!" Bailey told her, swiftly bending to hug her.

"I'm not," Baby insisted.

"How about you be my princess for the day, then?" Michael scooped the sticky child up so she could see the stage better, and positioned the other kids in front of the entourage of Bailey, Cora and the cowboys. "Now I've got a court of princes and princesses." He glanced sidelong at Bailey.

Bailey's smile froze at the look in Michael's eyes. It was warmer than the way he looked at anyone else. "What am I?" she asked softly.

"Someone special," he said simply.

There had to be something she could say to that, *something,* but she was so surprised she couldn't think of the proper reply. Michael had never murmured endearments to her before! Not in the light of day, and not so certain of his words.

"Dixons. Wades." Gunner came to stand beside Bailey. She could feel Michael's whole body tighten.

"King," he replied in kind.

"Now we've got a king to add to your court, Mr. Michael!" Baby cried with delight.

Michael didn't say a word. Gunner ruffled Baby's hair and nodded to Cora. "Looks like Brad's got everything going for him today."

Her insides pitching from worry over poor Brad's showing, and Michael talking to her so sweetly and Gunner standing next to them having once offered to marry her, Bailey couldn't make her lips move to answer. Fortunately, Mr. Day came to the microphone. His daughter stood beside him, beaming, proud to have everyone's attention on her. In back of them, on the large stage, the touted masterpiece was veiled under thick velvet.

Every ounce of Bailey went tense. Her chin was set as she watched her brother take his place beside Deenie and her father. What if no one bid on Brad's supposed masterpiece?

"As ya'll may have noticed today, Fallen, Texas, has been hiding a very bright light under its bushel basket. But not any longer. We are proud to introduce Brad Dixon to the country at large as the most celebrated artist of his time!''

Brad blushed beet red under his blond hair. Deenie clung to his arm. Nearby, a TV camera rolled, a city station obviously called in by Mr. Day. Bailey thought she might be ill. She rubbed her arms before clutching the children in front of her. She was terribly conscious of Gunner on one side of her, Michael on the other. Michael briefly touched his hand to hers, giving her a sensation of security, if only for a second.

"Do you want to do the honors, Brad?" Mr. Day asked.

"You go ahead, sir." Brad's voice had dwindled to a terrified whisper.

"All right. Deenie, grab the other end," her father instructed. Together they lifted the royal crimson covering, revealing the canvas to a breathless, craning crowd.

Bailey's mind registered one split image—hands that had come up to clap and possibly to bid on the painting suddenly paused in midair. The air went eerily still, then her ears filled with the sound of raucous laughter.

Chapter Twelve

Bailey froze. Deenie stood motionless, her stiff hair and clingy evening gown still, mannequin-like.

Everyone stared at the brilliantly colored likeness of Deenie, which wasn't a likeness at all. Not one anyone in Fallen expected.

It was the three faces of Eve come to life. A blond fall of hair swept Picasso-like into three faces all shaded into one, one blank, one with only a smile, the last with only an eye, which gazed somewhere far in the distance. Somehow, the faces melded together in a blend that was riveting and harmonious. The faces swept into the lines of an elegant neck and then a model's body, which wore a sapphire-blue gown. Deenie's gown.

But the stunning gown was pushed up to her bare thighs, revealing long, lovely legs as the woman stood in a field of dry, blowing yellow grasses. On her feet were not beaded evening shoes, as Deenie wore now, but boots, scruffy cowboy boots, which Deenie might once have worn in a rodeo parade but never, ever with a glittering evening gown.

Because the townspeople knew Deenie Day, the portrait was humorous. She wouldn't be caught dead with her skirt bunched—the dress was too expensive—though she might definitely flaunt her charms. It was a perfect juxtaposition of Deenie's personalities, though Brad had presented her face so that a person who had never met her wouldn't recognize her. The rendering was haunting and ethereal, lyrical and provocative.

But to the citizens of Fallen, having listened to Deenie brag for weeks about the masterpiece that might make her a star, it was a great cause for laughter.

"What are you laughing at?" Deenie cried suddenly. "Why are you laughing at me?"

Bailey bowed her head. Poor Brad looked horrified that his art was receiving such mocking hilarity. And she wouldn't have wished this on Deenie for anything, not that anyone was really laughing at Deenie, but at her grand expectations.

"I've done nothing to be made fun over!" Deenie screeched. "Stop it right now!"

Folks shifted uncomfortably, but their faces still showed their mirth. Mr. Day stood by, staring at the portrait he'd commissioned. He wasn't laughing but seemed rather confused, as if he admired it and wasn't sure why it was being scorned.

Deenie ran to the front of the stage, staring wrathfully at her subjects. "You shouldn't be laughing at me. I've done nothing to be ridiculed for or to be ashamed of! If you want to shame someone, it should be her!"

Bailey glanced up, to her horror discovering Deenie's finger pointing righteously at her. Michael and Gunner stiffened beside her.

"Why do you not make fun of her? She's pregnant

and unmarried. Why is it always Bailey the good who can do no wrong, but you laugh at me when I would never do such a...wrong thing!''

Bailey's mouth fell open. The children turned to stare at her in shock, as did all of Fallen's townspeople. Deenie smiled, delighted that the focus of scorn had shifted from her.

''I—I—'' Bailey stuttered, unable to say anything more.

The waiting silence was deafening. All she could think of was that Brad must have told Deenie. But no, Brad looked as stunned as Bailey. In fact, he looked furious as he stormed off the stage. Frightened, Bailey glanced at Michael, but he was staring at her like he couldn't possibly have heard right.

''Hang on just a dad-blasted minute!'' Cora Wade exclaimed. ''I've been in that house with Bailey, and I'm willing to state that there has been no untoward behavior whatsoever. How dare you question my reputation, Deenie Day?''

''Sorry, Cora, but the bun was baking long before you came back to Fallen, though I must say, *your* presence certainly gave folks plenty to speculate about,'' Deenie retorted.

Suddenly, Gunner's strong voice resonated over the audience. ''It's really no one's business, Deenie, if Bailey and I haven't made it to the altar as fast as you deem proper.''

Bailey gasped, whirling to face Gunner. He stared at her, willing her, it seemed, to be strong.

''If Bailey's expecting, it's mine,'' Michael said in a loud, firm voice.

Bailey gasped again, whipping around to face Michael.

"My, it does seem as though you've been busy, Bailey. Two men, and both wealthy as all get out! Of course, in your desperate circumstances, perhaps that's necessary," Deenie stated, her taunting voice like a whip. "Who would have ever thought such fierce rivals as the Kings and the Wades had one thing in common, and living conveniently between them for sharing?"

"Deenie!" her father exclaimed. "That's enough!"

"Well, Daddy," she countered in a sugar-sweet tone, "you shouldn't have fallen for Bailey's pious, we-mustn't-accept-charity attitude. You've always said the Dixons are such hard-working folk who simply missed out on life's good breaks, but as you can see, they're only panhandlers preying on people's sympathy. Now you see the truth."

"I certainly do," he snapped, dragging his daughter by the arm down the stage steps.

Bailey felt hundreds of eyes upon her, assessing Deenie's words. She felt ill with humiliation.

"Come on," Gunner commanded. "Let's get her out of here."

"Don't tell me you're trying to help," Michael stated.

"Look, Michael, Bailey is more important than your pride. Take her home, and I'll bring the kids."

"No," Bailey said through clenched teeth. "I'm not leaving."

"What?" the men's startled voices asked in unison.

"I'm not running," Bailey stated. "This is Brad's big day, and I'm no traitor to be running off when things get uncomfortable."

"Bailey—" Michael began.

"I'm a stayer, not a goer," she said, planting her

feet, though both men had one each of her arms in their hands to propel her for a quick escape. "And I'm no coward. Let Deenie say what she likes, I'm not ashamed of anything I've done. And I'm not leaving my brother when he needs me."

Bidding erupted for the now truly infamous painting. The auctioneer talked loud and fast, eagerly watching hands in the crowd indicating increased amounts.

"Are you certain?" Michael asked.

"Of course I am." She stared at him. "You can't really believe I'd desert my brother. Look at his face."

Indeed, he appeared crestfallen. This should be his greatest moment, the culmination of all his hard work, as the auctioneer called higher and higher numbers. Yet Brad was totally oblivious. Bailey's heart went out to him. She knew the feeling of heartbreak, and there was no quick suture for a heart that was tearing in two. She pulled away from Michael and Gunner and hurried to the stage steps where Brad stood, staring blankly after Deenie, being marched off ignominiously by her irate father.

"Oh, Brad, I'm so sorry!"

Bailey's voice seemed to pull him to the present. He smiled at her sadly. "I am, too."

They hugged each other, staying wrapped in the security they'd shared for the months since their parents had died.

"I've done you wrong, Bailey."

"How could you possibly ever do me wrong?" She looked at her handsome, devastated brother.

"By loving her," he whispered. Then he met her worried eyes. "I didn't tell her, Bailey. I promise."

"I believe you." She rested her head against Brad's chest, closing her eyes. But how had Deenie known?

Instantly, she thought of the ragged boots the woman in the painting wore. They seemed very familiar, as if she'd seen them before, though not so scuffed.

Then she remembered. Those brown boots had been hanging over the edge of the sofa the night she'd gone to tell Michael about the baby. Not Michael but Deenie had heard her anguished words.

Michael's boots were larger. He would never have thrown himself into such a casual position on the leather sofa. In the darkness, she hadn't gauged size nor anything else, simply registering that Michael didn't speak. Of course, Michael had always been taciturn, so she hadn't been surprised.

The only surprise in this matter was that Deenie had managed to keep her news bulletin to herself this long.

"I brought this on you. I selfishly said you shouldn't have messed with Michael because he'd never marry you. Look who *I* fell for! I can't make a good decision to save my life," Brad said, his voice ripped by distress. "And now I've ruined yours."

"Brad, nothing is ruined. If these people weren't my real friends before, I don't need them now. We've sold the land. We can sell the house and move away. Forget about it," she soothed. "Do you hear that? The bidding is so high I must be misunderstanding the auctioneer. Listen to the sound of your success!"

"You're not misunderstanding." Michael came to stand beside them. "Those taxes are going to get paid off, after all."

She stared into Michael's worry-lined face and questioning eyes. *He hadn't known about the baby.*

"I don't know what to say to you," she murmured, "except that I'm sorry."

"Don't be. Sorry's a waste of time." He took a deep, sighing breath. "If anyone's sorry, it ought to be me." A wry grin etched his face. "Guess I shouldn't have waited so long, but...I suppose we'll get married now."

Her heart beat faster, harder, painfully. "What do you mean?"

"If you're expecting, we'll do the right thing by the child," he said, his tone practical.

Bailey pulled herself up tall, her spine rigid with pride.

"Sold, for one million dollars!" the auctioneer cried. "To the big spender from California, whose wallet we welcome to Fallen with open arms!"

"The *hell* we will," Bailey declared over the amazed clapping of the spectators, never unlocking her gaze from Michael's. "I wouldn't dream of marrying a man who thinks he's going to do the right thing by me! If I was looking to be saved, Michael Wade, I would have married Gunner a long time ago when he asked me!"

Michael swiveled to stare at his rival. "What has Gunner got to do with anything?"

"Plenty," Bailey shot back. "If I wanted the honorable thing done by me, I'd have immediately taken Gunner up on his offer because I knew you wouldn't be caught dead or alive at an altar."

"How did he know you were pregnant?" Michael growled. "You said you never saw him while you were working."

"I told him just before I told you—er, thought I'd told you. I was horribly ill at his house the morning I went to see about the job, and he was so worried about me that I felt I needed to explain that I wasn't truly ill with anything catching.''

Beside them, Brad accepted delighted congratulations from people who'd known him all his life and were happy to see one of their own make good. The children and Cora and the cowboys sidled up to the trio, who were clearly at odds.

''Maybe this should be discussed at a later date,'' Cora suggested. ''Nothing's going to be solved right away, and it is Brad's big moment.''

''We'll discuss it now,'' Michael said, ''and I better get a good answer as to why Gunner's name is even being mentioned in reference to marrying you, Bailey Dixon!''

She gasped. ''Are you insinuating…how dare you?''

''Hold on, Michael,'' Gunner interrupted. ''I know you aren't listening to yourself or you'd regret what you just implied. Keep that temper under that hat of yours.''

''C'mon, boss,'' Fred said, taking Gunner forcibly by the arm. ''You cain't do any good arguing with a stubborn stumphead of a man.''

Bailey was relieved when Gunner nodded. ''Call me if you need me, Bailey,'' he said.

''I will.'' She met Michael's eyes. ''Though I'm positive I can handle this myself.'' Her tone was determined. She turned to hug her brother without another glance at Michael. He could offer to give her heaven on a cloud right now and she wouldn't dream of accepting. She knew just how Brad felt.

What a fool I've been.

Suddenly, she couldn't stay another moment around

Michael. Now that she knew Brad's painting had sold for an astonishing price, she could escape. "Wait, Fred," she called, "do you have enough room in your truck for me and the children?"

"I'll ride in the back with the kids," Gunner offered. "You and Baby sit up front with Fred, since he's driving."

"Thanks. Goodbye, Brad. We'll celebrate when you get home." Bailey was breathless as she ushered the children into the black truck. She didn't care what anyone in Fallen thought—she couldn't handle another moment of being on display with Michael. Not when it felt like her heart was being torn right out of her.

TWO HOURS LATER, Michael sat in his den trying to figure out what had happened. The Dixons' roof was finished and secure, and they had packed and disappeared before he'd returned. If he'd known today was going to blow up in his face, he wouldn't have hired the extra work crew. He'd feel better if Bailey was in his house so he'd have a better shot at catching her. He *had* to talk to her.

He wasn't sure he'd ever been this confused. For a man who prided himself on his iron control, he felt as though his brain had the consistency of warm candle wax.

"Want to talk?"

He barely glanced up as his mother entered the room. "Not really."

"All right." She went out as silently as she'd entered.

Michael sighed. Gunner King, of all people. Bailey should have known better than to stir up that hornet's nest. If she wanted to favor Gunner's proposal, then she could by golly help herself.

He wasn't going to be done the way his mother had done his father by making cow eyes at Sherman King. He'd never be jealous of anything King, and he'd sure as shooting never be jealous over a woman. Bailey wasn't going to push that particular button because as far as he was concerned, he'd done everything he could to make her happy.

If she wasn't, so be it.

But if she was carrying his child, he'd fight to the death over that. No King was raising anything of *his*.

"Someone's at the door!" Cora called. "Do you want me to answer it?"

"If you don't mind." He sat on the edge of the sofa. Maybe it was Bailey. Could be she wanted to patch things up between them.

Gunner King strode into the room. Michael instantly rose.

"Wade," Gunner said without so much as a hello, "I'm gonna whip your hide until it's not even fit for shoe leather."

Chapter Thirteen

Any rational judgment that might have been left in Michael's mind dissipated instantly. "I'm more than happy to take you on, King, any time you like."

"Put 'em up, then." Gunner instantly adopted a boxing stance.

"Hold it!" Cora cried, running between them. "Let's not do this! We've managed to avoid an all-out war for years. There's no point in losing blood about anything now."

"Move, Mother," Michael commanded.

"Mrs. Wade, pardon me, but if you don't mind moving just a little to the right, I can knock the bejesus out of your son so fast he'll not even feel the pain."

"I'll be damned if you will," Michael stated.

Cora dispensed a fast, equal kick to each man's kneecap. Both men grunted and edged away from her swiftly.

"Damn it, Mother!" Michael had no idea his mother could kick so hard, but she was wearing boots and obviously hadn't spared either her guest or her son.

"Don't you cuss me, Michael Wade." She stared at both of them angrily. "I've had all of this I'm going to take. If your fathers didn't come to blows, then this generation isn't going to, either, unless I'm the one dispensing them." Taking a deep breath, she nodded. "Now, then, Gunner, what brings you to our house?"

"Bailey Dixon." He gritted the words out, feeling his kneecap gingerly.

"I guessed as much. Dixon's are always in the middle." She rolled her eyes. "You mentioned marriage to her in front of all of Fallen today."

"Yes, ma'am. But I was just trying to save her the humiliation because I realized your worthless son wasn't raising his hand on her behalf."

"Worthless!" Michael howled. "I didn't even know Bailey was expecting a baby."

"You didn't do right by her, Michael," Gunner said pointedly. "You shouldn't have—uh—"

"That's none of your business," Michael snapped. "If anybody's got a complaint to be filing, it ought to be coming from the Dixon household."

"Maybe not, but I'm making it my business. Brad's the head of that household, and we both know he can't give you the whupping you deserve. He'd damage his million-dollar hands, for one thing, and he wouldn't hurt a living creature, for another. Me, I've got neither of those reservations."

"Why is fighting with Michael going to solve anything?" Cora wanted to know. "He's willing to marry Bailey. She turned him down."

"Because he's too lazy and stubborn to court her the way she wants to be courted. She's loved you forever, you sorry sack. But your pride is the most important thing to you. She deserves better." Gunner thumped his chest. "I'll tell you something, Michael, I know how to please a woman. And if you can't make

Bailey happy, I'll be more than happy to do the job for you."

Michael forgot his smarting shin. "You...I'm going to kill you."

Cora shoved her hands against hard chests to keep the men apart.

"She sold me her land, Michael. I'd say you've got little left but your pride at this point. Happy?"

Michael stared at Gunner, whose brown eyes glinted like flint in the dimly lit room. "Why?"

"Why not? She needed the money. I need the water, and I can always use a little extra land." He shrugged, as if the whole matter meant little to him. "You'll have no water, no woman...no child. But, hey, what do you care, Michael? You'll have everything that makes you happy."

Gunner smiled, but it was a cold-blooded smile. Michael felt his mother clench the front of his shirt in her hands to keep him from leaping over her. Anger buzzed in his ears and pounded his pulse, longer, harder. "Stay away from Bailey," he said tightly.

"I don't think so. She's a great woman. Pretty, sweet, sexy—"

"Get out of my house, Gunner. Don't ever let me see your face again."

"Ah." Gunner cocked his head. "You don't want me to win Bailey. You'd just rather sit around your house feeling sorry for yourself and finally, when she's in desperate straits, you'll do her the big favor of marrying her, huh?" He laughed and put his brown hat on his head. "I tell you what, Michael. I've long wanted to wipe the Wades right out of my line of vision. I've got your water. Your cattle will have nothing to drink and you'll have to find another water source. I've even got one of your best ranch hands. This has all been just a matter of waiting for the right time to acquire what's offered to me. But now I've decided I want it all. So I'm going to court Bailey the way she should be." He smirked at Michael before nodding at Cora. "I'll try not to make you look too bad. Night, Cora."

Michael closed his eyes as Gunner left the room. He realized his teeth were locked together in a clench and slowly released them. Outside, he could hear Baby's lamb bleating and the Dixon children whooping. They were obviously celebrating Brad's big day. A miracle had reached down out of heaven and saved the Dixon family. He was glad for them, but he wished he were outside with them.

He rubbed his chin, realizing he wasn't angry with Gunner.

He was lonely.

And he wouldn't have seen red so fast over Gunner's threats if his rival hadn't been right.

I do love Bailey. I didn't want to get married. But I do love her. And I don't want to lose her.

It was time to get down off the fence.

"DAMN! Ya'll nearly got me killed!" Gunner reprimanded the three men waiting in the bushes outside the Wade den. "Do you know it was all Cora could do to keep that lug off of me?"

"Ya did fine, boss," Fred said proudly. The four of them skulked away from the ledge and hustled down the back of the property, leaping over concealing shrubbery so they could walk to Gunner's and talk privately. "We heard every word," Fred said, puffing.

"I thought smoke was gonna shoot right out the top of Michael's head," Chili gloated.

"Smoke! Try fire!" Curly chuckled to himself as he hurried along.

"I hope this works," Gunner said worriedly. "I've done everything I can to move that ol' hoss along, but damn! I may end up marrying Bailey, after all, if he doesn't get a move on!"

"Nope," Fred said with certainty. "You got Michael's boots moving now. Trust me, he's got a competitive spirit. And he does like Bailey. He just needed a spur stuck to him." He grinned, rubbing his palms together in delight. "And you've got the satisfaction that you beat him all along, and he didn't even know it!" They all high-fived each other. "Yes," Fred cried jubilantly, "Michael's hand has been forced. And force is the only thing that gets two immovable objects together, which makes a straight line, and then the heart will wander no more!"

"The recipe of love," Chili said with an exultant sigh.

Gunner shook his head. "If you ask me, it sounds like a recipe for *disaster*. Shoot, it doesn't feel like I'm winning. Are you sure I'm winning?" he asked Fred.

"Aw." Fred glanced at Gunner. "Hey, I heard there was a new girl in town. Some girl from New York. Maybe you oughta talk to her."

"Sure," Gunner said on a snort. "That's all I need, a Yankee lady from New York City."

"I don't know. I heard she was real pretty. And can ride rings around barrels." Chili stopped at Gunner's porch. "Speaking of riding, I wonder if ol' man Day put his daughter in a cage where she belongs?"

They all shook their heads over the thought and went into Gunner's house for a well-deserved beer.

DEENIE WAS NOT in a cage. She might as well have been.

"I blew it," she murmured to the stars, which were just beginning to light the darkening sky outside her window.

Not only had she ruined her father's big showing, she'd made a laughingstock of herself. Worse than that, as ashamed as she was of her behavior, had been the expression on Brad's face as her father led her away.

He had looked shattered.

She had done that to him.

"I FEEL BAD that my big day turned out so horribly for you," Brad told his sister.

Bailey gave him a brave smile. "Just worry about yourself, Brad."

They were silent for a few moments as they sat in the kitchen, watching the children frolic in the yard outside the window.

"I wish I could be as carefree as they are." Brad smiled ruefully. "They never have to worry about tax bills…"

"Or broken hearts," Bailey continued for him. "I can't believe my brother is a millionaire."

"I'm *not*. If we had a million, it would be the Dixons who were finally worth good money after years of being poor folks, not me."

They laughed together at the twist of fate.

"But since ol' Uncle Sam's got his hand in our pocket, don't guess any of us can claim to be rich.

He'll get most. Still, I'm so grateful, Bailey." Brad smiled at her. "I will admit it was awe-inspiring, electrifying, crazy, when I heard the auctioneer say *sold* for a million dollars."

"I was sure I hadn't heard right. Brad, can you believe it? You're going to be famous." Bailey still had to pinch herself to make certain she wasn't in a dream. *The tax bill would be paid.*

"Deenie's the famous one. Mr. Day called again to thank me tonight—I should be thanking him. He apologized for the thousandth time about what Deenie did…" Brad couldn't quite meet Bailey's eyes. "Then he mentioned that the guy from California does something in TV or commercials. They want Deenie to do a print ad for ladies' razors." He winced. "She does have real pretty legs."

"Oh, Brad." Bailey didn't know what to say.

"I guess the problem with Deenie is she's pretty on the outside but rotten on the inside. So I'm glad she's getting what she wants. She'll be away from Fallen, and that's what she wanted more than anything. And I won't have to wonder if I'm going to run into her every time I'm at Mr. Day's store."

"It's for the best, I'm sure." Bailey knew she spent an awful lot of time looking for Michael, in case he chanced to be outside when she was. Wondering made matters that much more difficult on the heart.

Wishing he'd show up on her porch had been a fruitless occupation. "Who would have ever dreamed we'd finally have enough money but not enough love?"

He laughed. "A complete reversal of our lives. Mom and Dad never saw a million in their whole lives, but we never knew for lack of love, did we?"

"No." And that's exactly what she wanted for her babies, she thought wistfully. A father who loved them. A mother who loved them. A household full of love. "Congratulations, Brad," she said, getting up to kiss her brother on the forehead. "I'm sorry we had to celebrate your big success with fizzy grape juice."

"I don't think I'm in danger of developing champagne taste, Bailey. I'm sure Deenie cured me of any chance of that happening. Anyway, babies are more reason to celebrate than money, so I'd rather do without the champagne."

He got up, too. They went outside to join the children and look at the half curve of moon pasted in the dark velvet sky. Heaven was so far away, Bailey thought. She glanced over her shoulder at the Walking W.

Almost as far away as Michael.

BAILEY NEARLY SCREAMED when a big figure sat on her bed that night, waking her.

"Sh! It's me!"

"Michael! What in the world are you doing?" Bailey sat up, trying to see him. All that was visible was a black hulk on the edge of her bed. "Let me turn on the lamp."

"No. I'm only staying a second, and then I want you to rest."

"Oh, right. You scare me half to death and then I'm supposed to get right back to sleep. What are you doing in my room? How did you get in the house?"

Michael chuckled softly. "One, it's my turn to pay the nighttime visits. Two, it was easy to get in the house. Your folks always kept a key at our house in case one of the kids accidentally locked Polly outside while she was gardening or hanging laundry or something.''

''Well, that could happen easily enough. I keep a key under a rock just in case.''

They were silent for a moment. ''So. I guess you had something on your mind?'' she asked.

''I've got something on my mind, Bailey. You.''

She liked the sound of that. ''Is there any reason you can't say it in the light of day? Have you been drinking? Too scared to face me except under cover of darkness?''

''No to all of your questions. It was my turn to visit, is all. I've been meaning to ask you, why did you quit coming around, anyway?''

She swallowed. ''When I found out I was pregnant, I...I just needed some time to think, I guess. I didn't know what you'd say.''

She felt him shift on the bed. Light cologne filtered to her, and the scent of a freshly washed shirt.

''It's a shock, but I wish you'd told me. I didn't much like the way I found out.''

It was pointless to say that she thought she had told him. If she hadn't been so afraid of him not wanting her, she might have collared him at some point and asked him why he wasn't more interested in talking about the baby. The specter of him offering to marry her because of the baby had loomed too darkly for her. ''I'm sorry, Michael. But I guess that's all water under the bridge now.''

''Mostly. Except Gunner came to see me tonight.''

Michael on her bed, so close to her, made her think about all the times they'd made love in the darkness. Bailey didn't want to think about Gunner.

''He gave me a may-the-best-man-win challenge.''

She couldn't stand talking to him without seeing him, so she flipped on her bedside lamp before he could stop her. He had the most worried scowl on his face she'd ever seen.

But he was so darn attractive in blue jeans, boots and a red-and-black plaid flannel shirt that she almost wished she hadn't turned on the light. Except then she would have missed seeing how the bones of his cheeks stood out as he grimaced, and the way his dark hair lay against his collar.

And, of course, that wonderful scowl. "What's the matter with that? Don't you think you're the best man?" she teased.

He stared at her, his gaze intense. "I want to be the *groom,* damn it."

Chapter Fourteen

Bailey's smile slipped away. "You're saying that because of the baby."

"Of course I'm saying it because of the baby. I don't know who's hit the bigger jackpot, me or Brad." Michael swallowed. "I'm not even sure it's hit me that I'm going to be a father yet. I keep thinking, how can I be a father? There's a little person who's going to need me."

"Two," Bailey murmured.

"Too?" He stared at her. "Well, of course you'll need me. That's why I'm here."

She paused, realizing he'd misunderstood her but not liking what he'd said. "I don't want you to marry me because you think I'm going to need you. I don't need you, Michael."

He held up a hand. "Well, not in the financial sense anymore."

"I never needed you in the financial sense!"

"Oh, come on, Bailey, you know what I mean."

Pulling the covers to her chin, she said, "No, I don't."

He sighed. "Why do you have to make this so difficult?"

"Because it is difficult!"

"Okay. But it doesn't have to be. We don't have to argue and feel bad over this. It's simple. We're going to have a baby. So we're going to get married."

"It's not that simple!" she hissed. "I'm not getting married just because I'm pregnant!"

Michael blew out an exasperated sigh, then his lips momentarily flattened as he stared at her. "Look. I never pretended that I wanted to get married. You didn't seem to expect flowers and chocolate hearts from me. I thought you were happy. Frankly, I don't know exactly what it is that you want."

She hesitated, her gaze searching his face. When she saw that he did appear to be confused, she nodded. "All right, I'll tell you. I want you to get out of my bedroom."

"What? What did I say?"

"It's what you don't say, Michael. I advise you to go now, before you make everything worse than it is."

"Bailey—"

"No." She held up a hand. "I'm not going to play the stupid emotional game of checkmate your parents played all their marriage."

"This has nothing to do with them."

"It has everything to do with them. Look at how you treat your mother!"

He frowned, his brows drawn low on his forehead. "She has nothing to do with this. She left a long time ago, and as far as I'm concerned, she might as well have stayed gone."

Sadness crept into Bailey. "You're so unforgiving, Michael. You don't realize it, but you're weighing down your ability to be an emotional partner in our relationship."

"You sound like you've been talking to Fred." Michael shook his head. "He's been blabbering all kinds of weird stuff ever since he got sick."

Bailey shook her head. "I'm not blabbering, it's not weird stuff, and I don't need a rock like you sitting on my heart crushing my soul. I've had a life-changing experience, and I'm seeing everything in a different light."

He snorted. "A million dollars would probably make anyone see things in a different light."

"Michael, you're an ass. And I don't have time to talk to you anymore. I need my sleep. I've got to be at work in the morning, and I've got kids to take care of. Good night."

She lay down and turned on her side so she wouldn't have to look at him.

"Why are you still working at Gunner's? With such a windfall, you can quit his silly job. All he did, Bailey, was figure out a way to get money to you without injuring your pride. But you don't need money anymore."

"Good night, Michael."

He was silent for a moment. "I sure didn't think it was necessary for you to sell him the water rights. You know he's not going to let me use any of the water now. I don't suppose there's an outside chance you haven't signed any papers yet and would consider selling the land to me?"

She jumped up, landing on the floor so swiftly that he drew back in surprise. Flinging open her bedroom door, she said, "Get out now before I call Brad."

He held up his hands in surrender. "Okay, okay." Walking to her, he stared at her. "Bailey, don't you think the pregnancy is making you a little emotional, maybe? A little touchy?''

"No, I don't.'' She gritted the words out. "But as I said, it's making me see a lot of things in a whole new light.'' Glaring at him, she poked one finger squarely in the middle of his broad chest. "I want to make certain you've heard exactly what I said to you tonight, Michael. I said I've had a life-altering experience, which has made me rethink things. Life-altering is not Brad's paintings selling. It's not selling water rights and land so that the Dixons can stand on their own multiple feet. It's learning that I'm having twins.''

Shock chased disbelief across his face. "Twins?''

"That's right. Trouble times two where you're concerned.''

Briskly, she closed the bedroom door.

TWINS! If the floor opened up beneath him and he dropped through the first-floor ceiling, Michael couldn't feel more shaken. He was going to be the father of two little children! Not one, but two. It had been difficult enough to imagine one tot running through his quiet, staid bachelor abode. But two! And Dixon blood in them. They'd be wild, unruly. There would be pet lambs, at the minimum, and who only knew what other tortures unleashed upon him. He'd just reconciled himself to learning to deal with one, but two!

"Bailey, I think I feel sick,'' he said through the door.

"Put your head between your knees,'' she advised.

"I can't stop taking breaths. I might be hyperventilating.''

"Paper bags are in the kitchen."

He leaned against the wall to steady himself. "Are you sure it's twins?"

There was no answer for a moment. Then she said, "Yes, Michael. Unless Doc Watson's seeing double."

He was seeing double. "How are we going to raise two kids?"

A sarcastic snort erupted from Bailey. "I've been raising five. I imagine two more will be a piece of cake."

"Maybe to you, but I haven't had any practice." He hadn't even had siblings to spar with. His family bond hadn't been strong, either. He was a loner.

Not anymore. "Bailey?"

"Yes?"

"I know I've got some things to resolve, but…in the meantime, will you make me a promise?" He put his forehead against the cool wall.

"I doubt it."

That didn't surprise him. He really couldn't ask her to make promises on his behalf. "Don't marry Gunner. Please?"

Silence.

He'd about given up hope of hearing her voice again, his blood pounding in his ears, his heart racing at the thought of her moving on with her life. Moving away from him.

"I can safely promise you that."

Grateful beyond words, he closed his eyes. "Good night. Get some rest."

"Good night."

Shoving away from the wall, Michael stumbled down the stairs like a drunk. He locked the door behind him and made it to his truck.

Snatching open the door, he jumped a foot when he realized three cowboys were sitting inside his truck, blowing on their fingers to keep them warm.

"What the hell are you doing?" he shouted, completely rattled.

"Making sure you didn't overstay your welcome," Fred told him.

Irate, Michael demanded, "What does that mean?"

"It means, boss," Chili explained, "that you ought not be getting second helpings of the milk before you buy it, as they say. You had five more minutes before we threw rocks at Bailey's window."

"Since when did you appoint yourselves my chaperons?"

Curly stared at him sagely. "Since we realized you needed our assistance."

"I don't need anyone's assistance." Boy, what a lie that was. He needed help real bad. He was just so shell-shocked he didn't know what kind of help he ought to be looking for.

"What's the matter, boss?" Chili asked. "You look kind of poorly."

"I feel poorly," Michael moaned. "I'm having twins!"

SUNDAY MORNING bloomed bright and early, but Michael hadn't slept all night, so morning or night didn't matter much to him. He sat at the kitchen table, freshly showered, in a suit and drinking coffee.

He gazed at the clock on the wall steadily. The clock had hung in the kitchen since he was a child. It had morning glories and triangle-shaped leaves twining among the numbers. The flowers didn't interest him, but the black, scrolling numbers did.

At eight-thirty, he got up, washed his mug out and put it away. Then he went outside and got into his father's Lincoln town car, which he allowed to warm for a few moments in the early light of the freezing February morning.

When he deemed it warm enough inside for the children, he backed out of his drive and headed up the Dixon's drive. Leaving the car running, he got out, went to the porch and rang the doorbell.

Baby answered, as always. "Baby, is Bailey around?"

"No."

His brows raised. "Where is she?"

"She went to church with Mr. Gunner."

"What?" His heart free-fell into his boots.

"Hello, Michael," Brad said, coming to stand behind Baby. "Bailey's not here."

"I heard." Michael grunted. "I was going to offer her a ride to church."

Brad grinned. "I don't think she was expecting you."

"No, she wasn't." As little as he liked to admit it, Gunner had sneaked up and bushwhacked him. "Want a ride?"

Brad looked at him curiously. "You're still going?"

"I've a mind to. No rule that says two men who like the same woman can't sit in the same church, is there?"

"Um, I don't guess so...."

Michael smiled. "So. You want a ride or not?"

After a second, Brad nodded. "Sure beats riding in the pickup. And I might be needed for bodyguard duties."

He snorted. "Who for?"

Brad shook his head. "I'm thinking maybe for you, if Bailey doesn't want to see you."

That worried Michael. "She's going to be seeing a lot of me. She'd better decide she likes it."

Her brother laughed out loud. "Michael, I could use lessons from you in the bullheaded department."

"Well." He wasn't sure what to think about that. "I could probably use some lessons from you in the, uh, sensitive department. Bailey seems to think I'm a bit rough around the edges."

Brad clapped him on the back as the children filed past them out the door. "Diamonds start out rough around the edges, too, and look how they turn out. Ever thought about buying my sister a diamond, by the way?"

Astounded, Michael stared at Brad.

Brad shrugged, grinning as he locked the door. "Just something to think about."

He hesitated briefly. "I got the distinct impression marrying me wasn't the most inviting thought to Bailey at this moment."

They walked to the car together, where the children waited. Arms flailed, and children's voices alternated between bickering and laughter. Brad closed the car door they'd left open.

"It's just a guess on my part, Michael, a hunch. But my sister was humiliated pretty well in front of the entire town of Fallen. Those that weren't at the square on Saturday heard about the whole thing before sundown. No doubt the excitement will even receive some attention in the Fallen *Gazette*'s gossip column."

He got in the passenger side door, and Michael slid into the driver's side. Baby buckled her seat belt in her place between them.

"So," Brad continued, "she's at church with Gunner, and you're fixing to show up there, too, and you both already offered to marry her in front of Fallen, so both of you sitting with her today is likely to really set the talk on fire."

"I see your point." Michael hadn't thought about aiming the spotlight at himself or Bailey. He'd merely been thinking about going to church with her, which seemed like a gentlemanly thing to do and a way to score good marks with her. "How does a diamond fit into all of this?"

"It fits in this way. As Bailey's big brother, and the uncle of the twins we'll be seeing this summer, I'm finally saying what I should have said but which Bailey asked me not to. I know you think I'm a sensitive male, but sensitive's not synonymous with cowardly. Get an engagement ring on Bailey so folks will know she's going to have a husband, and let's not keep adding to the circus attraction we're becoming." His face was grim and un-Bradlike suddenly. "If you've heard of shotgun weddings, Michael, you can consider a cannon aimed on the Walking W."

MICHAEL WAS under siege. Gunner was threatening him with a best-man-wins challenge, Bailey was insisting she wouldn't marry him, and now Brad was cornering him for the knockout punch. His three employees weren't exactly in his corner, nor was his mother. They were all acting as chaperons and protectors of Bailey, like he was the villain.

He'd never been so ganged up on. He'd never been so unpopular. Once upon a time, he'd been left alone. Everything had changed. It was all fine and good for everyone to be on his case, but the problem was, Bailey was the immovable object. She wouldn't budge an inch. How the heck he could get an engagement ring on her finger was a puzzle he didn't have all the pieces to.

Sighing despondently, he drove the suddenly quiet Dixon clan to church.

He was not looking forward to yet another sermon.

BAILEY HEARD the gasps behind her and stiffened. She was kneeling in her customary place, the front pew of the church. Her heart suddenly pounding, she abbreviated her prayer and turned to look at what was causing the sudden commotion in the normally serene country church.

Brad and the children marched down the aisle, except for Baby, who had somehow wormed her way into being carried by Michael. Bailey jerked back to face the altar. Gunner shifted in his seat. Excited whispers assaulted her ears from all directions. To be the subject of such intense interest mortified her. A vision of her parents looking down, saddened by their unmarried, pregnant daughter's humiliation, forced her eyes tightly, urgently shut.

Please let this be the fastest hour of my life!

Michael seated himself next to her. Brad and the children took seats behind them. Just when Bailey thought her family couldn't possibly be more of a neon flashing sign in the sanctuary, a complete hush fell over the congregation.

Deenie Day sat beside Brad.

"I'm praying you can forgive me," she said quietly.

Chapter Fifteen

The service began, and the Dixons, Deenie, Michael and Gunner endured the next hour in discomfort.

Deenie thought Brad looked none too pleased to see her.

Gunner wasn't thrilled that his rival had managed to make it to church when he had fair and square gotten the jump on him.

Bailey felt she'd never been such a spectacle of mishap, with a bachelor on either side of her, a pew full of children who couldn't sit still today to save their souls and a rodeo queen who'd done her best to ruin Bailey's reputation.

For his part, Michael tried not to think about Bailey's warmth next to him. He was still in dire amazement that he was fathering twins, and just the thought of that made him realize how urgently he needed to get Bailey to an altar.

If only the stubborn woman would go there with him. He was in a terrible fix. To his dismay, the homily was on the beauty of marriage, and he'd have bet half his cattle that the topic of the day had swiftly been changed once the priest saw him sitting in the front pew.

It was a downright unfortunate situation.

If that wasn't bad enough, Baby sneezed during the entire hour. It was clear Bailey was concerned about her. Loud achoos and whispered requests for tissues, which passed from Bailey to Baby in Michael's lap, kept everyone shifting without cease.

He was very glad when the service ended. Fully intending to take everybody to Miss Nary's Pancakes and Dairy, even graciously intending to allow Gunner to accompany them, he was greatly chagrined when Gunner and Bailey took Baby with them and left. Brad didn't have much to say to Deenie, who left the church parking lot, despondent. Brad didn't appear to be in much better shape. Michael sighed, highly self-conscious with all the emotional turmoil surrounding him.

Packing the rest of the children and Brad into his car, Michael offered to take them out. Brad quietly declined. Hunched in the passenger seat, he was a vision of pale dejection. Michael sighed again and drove home, knowing that he and Bailey were not one whit closer to a solution—or each other.

To his disgruntlement, his mother waited for him in the kitchen, her suitcase packed at her feet.

"What are you doing?" he asked.

"It's time for me to head back home," Cora replied. "I'm not needed here any longer."

Hesitating, he took a moment to register the shock he felt at her decision to leave. He started to say that there wasn't any reason for her to go rushing off, but he didn't know one thing about her life. For all he knew, she had a husband back home who wanted his wife to return. Michael didn't think he'd want Bailey gone from him for an extended period. Now that he faced his mother's departure, Michael realized he'd wasted a valuable chance to get to know his mother by stewing in his own resentment.

He hadn't yet thanked her for rushing to Bailey's defense when Deenie had blurted the secret in front of Fallen's citizens. Somewhere in the fog of consternation he'd experienced at abruptly learning he was an unwed father in front of hundreds of folks who'd known his family since before he was born, it had registered that his mother had willingly, immediately hollered out that nothing untoward had occurred during her chaperonage. Though she had rushed to defend him and Bailey, she had not once taken him to task over his behavior. She might wonder why her son had made her a grandmother without a wedding anywhere on the horizon, but she didn't question him. Silently loyal and supportive, she had waited for him to talk if he needed.

He needed to, but had been too stubborn and angry to do so. Now that she was leaving, Michael felt like he was losing something that mattered greatly to him.

"If you've got to go, I guess you've got to," he said gruffly.

She stared at him before nodding as if she accepted his words. He looked at her brilliant silver hair, her refined air, which might be mistaken for coolness, and her alert blue eyes. Suddenly he realized he was standing in a room with a woman he really didn't know. It was a strange, suspended feeling.

Whether it was right or wrong, or if he was being selfish, he didn't know. But he didn't want her to leave again. Not this way. He rubbed his neck. He scratched at a place on his face that wasn't necessarily itching. He cleared his throat.

"If you've no place pressing to be," he said, trying to look for all the world like his words were casual, "nobody's showing you the door."

She watched him, her eyes lighting with surprise. "I'm on no particular schedule. Just didn't want to be in the way."

He swallowed. "You're not in mine."

"Seems like you've got the Walking W running well enough," she observed.

"Could always use an experienced hand on the reins, though." Shifting in place, he wondered if there was more he should be saying to the woman who was his mother. She wasn't an employee. He wasn't asking her to stay because he needed help with the ranch. "Truth is, I've missed you. I know I haven't acted like it, but—"

"I rather enjoy being here," she swiftly interrupted. "You know, spring is coming. I remember how busy it is on the ranch. My cooking skills are rusty, but I like to think I can still fix up something edible. I think a border of flowers around the house would look rather pretty, too." Glancing at her hands, she seemed to choose her next words carefully. "Of course, I like to believe I could be some help to Bailey, should you think she would welcome that."

He smiled. "Stay, Mom."

She returned his smile. "All right, son."

They stood looking at each other for a long moment. Michael savored his mother's acquiescence to remain at the Walking W. *It wasn't because of me that she left,* he thought, relieved to the core of his soul. *She left because her love was unreturned. But I love her.*

I will never allow Bailey to think I don't love her.

"I've been meaning to say this, but it's not easy."

Her smile was rueful. "You had absolutely nothing to do with my leaving your father. In fact, you're the one reason I stayed as long as I did."

Stunned pleasure rushed through him in a swirling torrent. He desperately hoped the hard lump lodged in his throat didn't mean he'd cry. Tears had no place in this moment. He should be happy. *I am happy. I'm just sorry I forgot how much I love her.* "It was hard as hell growing up without you, Mom. I wish you could have stayed."

"I know." Cora's eyes grew sad and dark. "After your father passed, I realized he was who he was. I made as many mistakes as he did, wanting him to be a way he couldn't be. I always thought he…he didn't love me." She took a deep breath and glanced around the kitchen. "He changed so much after you were born. Your father was remote, unreachable. When he was home, he spent so much time staring out this window into the Dixons' yard I assumed he was pining after Polly. I asked him once if he was, but he didn't say a word, just shook his head."

For the first time, he saw his mother as a woman with real feelings and necessary emotions. Bailey said she wanted him to love her. Yet she didn't seem to understand that he did. "Reckon I've got some of my father in me." Oh, he hated to admit that. Michael Wade, Senior, had been a successful cattleman but a damn poor family man. There had been no family picnics, no family outings, no laughter. No closeness.

Cora slipped into a seat at the table and stared at her son. "You do, I suppose. But you've also got some of me to water his genes down."

They laughed, and Michael took the seat next to his mother.

"He was a hard man," she said after a moment. "When I fell in love with him, I thought I was the luckiest girl on earth. Your father was so handsome, so rough and tough that he could handle the wildest steer, yet courteous enough to open doors for me. One night, he'd brought me over here to watch TV with him and his folks. We didn't go into Dallas to see the pictures like people do nowadays." She smiled, her face lit with amused memory. "Anyway, that night one of the cowboys got hurt, and so Michael went out to see what he could do. The cowboy had broken his arm and passed out in the snow from the pain, so your father carried him up to the house so his mother could set it. And I fell head over heels in love. I know it's not the way it's done now. We'd call ol' Doc Watson or drive to the hospital, but you have to remember, back then, there was nothing out here in the sticks but the Dixons, the Kings and the Wades. And the Wades were a resilient, hardworking, successful ranching family." She smiled, the memory still bright. "I thought, this man can take care of me. He's strong. He's tough. And I wanted desperately to marry him." She shrugged at Michael. "Your father was strong and tough until the day he died."

"All the way through."

She nodded. "Yes. All the way through."

Michael felt sorry for his mother. He didn't think he'd ever seen his father say much to his wife, except maybe to list some chores that needed to be seen to. "I think I knew. I think I knew he was as hard with you as he was with me. But I wanted you to stay, and I guess I...hated it when you left."

"I know. But your father had the money, you'd been raised on this ranch all your life, it was what you loved to do. I would have taken you with me, but your father said no, that taking you away from your birth-right was the wrong thing to do, and I had no fight left in me. I went away to heal like a tired, sick dog, but…I'm so sorry, Michael.'' She put her hand slowly over his fist on the table. ''You know, spending this time at the ranch has given me a chance to get to know you some, and I've decided you're probably the best combination of your father and I.''

He chuckled. ''Thanks, Mom.''

''I'm lucky I had the fence-sitters calling to give me progress reports. They've been second fathers to you.''

Maybe more than that. ''I wish I'd known they knew where to find you.'' There were many times he would have called his mother just to hear her voice.

''Your father wouldn't have allowed it,'' she said, cutting across his thoughts with the truth. ''He was a hard man. Once he made his mind up to extract re-venge…''

There needed to be no more said. Michael's father had kept the angry fire burning all his life with Sher-man King. A wife who'd left him would be subject to every blast of hot wrath his father had in his body.

''But now that I've been here for a while, I think I know why he was always staring out the window into the Dixons' yard,'' she said quietly. ''I catch myself doing it plenty.''

He knew why he did it. ''The Dixons are always doing something.''

''Gosh, yes, it's like watching a rerun of an old-fashioned family sitcom, except in color instead of black-and-white. Sometimes they remind me of the Waltons, but not very often. Too loud.''

He grinned. ''I watch 'em, too.''

"Well, a body can't help it. It's like a party you can't exactly join in but which you just gotta watch. I think your father felt left out."

Michael raised a brow. "How?"

"Well, don't you? All that happiness. All that love." She looked at Michael, her expression serious. "I think it stumped your father. Here we had all the money but little love or happiness, and they're dirt poor, but happier people you'll never see. I think he was truly mystified by the difference a fence line makes." Patting his hand, she pulled away to stand up. A teapot on the stove sat hot for tea, and she poured out two mugs, managing a glance out the window at the Dixon property. "Of course, it wasn't the fence line. It was a different set of priorities. Different ideas of what matters in life."

He had often stood and surveyed all the comings and goings next door, noting the vibrancy and excitement himself. "I thought I liked being alone, but having them under my roof sort of changed my mind. I didn't think I could stand all the uproar, but now that it's gone, it's, well…"

"Too damned quiet."

He laughed. "Exactly."

"Well, there's only one thing to do about it. You've got to get them back under your roof." Cora drank from her mug, eyeing her son over the top.

"Brad suggested an engagement ring, but Bailey's already told me she wouldn't marry me. I got the impression I didn't ask her properly, though. She's not exactly convinced I love her."

"Hmm." She thought about that for a moment. "Well, I can tell you that's no way to start off a marriage, much less something you want to last forever."

Sadly, she shook her head. "I'm not the one to give you advice on what would change Bailey's mind. It's something you'll have to figure out on your own." She tapped his untouched mug. "I know she loves you. And that's what every mother really wants for her son, a woman who loves him for himself. Unconditionally. I'd like to see it work out between you two."

For the first time, he really smiled. "I love you, Mom." He leaned over to wrap an arm around her shoulders and hold her close.

"I love you, son," she whispered. "I'll never again let you think I don't. Never."

They held each other for a long moment.

"I'm real nervous about being a father, especially of twins," he stated quietly.

She held him tighter. "You'll do fine, even if you are going to have more children all at once than your father and I had in our entire lifetime."

Her faith made him smile. "I hope I'll do it right."

She pulled away and stared deeply into his eyes. "I don't believe you can do it wrong if you do it with enough love, Michael."

"I have enough love."

His mother smiled. "Prove it to Bailey, then, is my only advice."

MICHAEL FIGURED he'd not be too good with romance. He hadn't had a lot of practice, and what Bailey wanted from him was a big question mark. But he knew what he wanted from Bailey—marriage—and that was as good a place to start as any. After talking with his mother, he walked outside and discovered

Bailey's bedroom light was still on. He picked up a pebble and tossed it at her window.

He was delighted when she pushed up the glass and looked down at him.

"What are you doing?" she demanded.

"Looking for the man in the moon. Saw you were up, and decided I might as well chat with the woman who had so many kids she didn't know what to do."

"Very funny." Her tone was sarcastic, but she smiled. "I'm pleased to hear that you know your nursery rhymes."

"A very good thing for a man who's having twins." He loved the sight of Bailey in her nightgown. It was white and ruffled at the neckline, and as she crossed her arms on the windowsill, he appreciated the vision of feminine roundness peeking out above the lace. He scrambled to think of another rhyme, because he'd run through his repertoire with that one. "How about, I love your hair, I love your voice, if you'll marry me, I will rejoice?" He stared up earnestly. "I made that up in the time-honored tradition of the cowboy poet."

She laughed at him. "I'd call it more doggerel than poetry, but I like it."

That was a step in the right direction. "Care to give me something to rejoice about?"

Shaking her head, she said, "Give me another. I'm not quite convinced. Show me all you've got, cowboy."

"Now there's an invitation I'd love to interpret literally." He grimaced, thinking hard. "How about, I love your body, I love your mind, damn it, Bailey, please be mine?"

Giggles filtered down to him. He frowned. "Hey, if you say yes, every year I'll make one of those glue and construction paper hearts like Baby does, and write my poem on it. My own personal valentine message since I usually forget to buy cards.''

''I give the poem a ten,'' Bailey told him. ''I don't know why. Maybe because it was so you. Impatient and outspoken. But I don't know about receiving it every year.''

''Well, hey, I could think up something different by next year.''

She laughed, pushing back her blond hair. ''I've got to go to bed.''

''Don't go yet! I could get the guitar out of the bunkhouse and serenade you.''

''Thanks, Michael, but I'll pass tonight. I've got to work in the morning.''

He didn't like that at all. ''I don't think you ought to be working. I think you ought to be resting those sons of mine. They're going to keep you all tired out once they arrive. Stock up on what sleep you can get now.''

''I'm planning on letting you stay up with them at night,'' Bailey teased. ''And you're going to be so disappointed when they're girls.''

''I don't care what they are. I think I should move in tonight to practice getting up with them.''

''I meant, I'm planning on letting you have night duty with them at your house.''

The smile evaporated from his face. ''Oh, no, Bailey Dixon. That is not the way it is going to be. I can tell you that from the very core of my soul. We are not going to raise our children apart. You can marry me now, or you can marry me later, but you are going to marry me.''

''You're sure about that?''

"Hell, yes, I am!" He stared at her stubbornly. "No child of mine is going to be raised like that. Er, children. Mother running here, father going there—no, ma'am. Uh-uh. This fence line's coming *down*."

Chapter Sixteen

"The fence line is staying up," Bailey returned. The window slammed shut.

Michael's blood ran so cold it felt like February wind freezing his soul. *I've done it now. Me and my big mouth.*

The front door flew open and the sound of footsteps hurrying across the porch gave him sudden hope. Bailey appeared before him, clad in her nightgown. He swallowed uncomfortably. "You're going to catch your death of cold."

"Then come inside. I want to talk to you. Please."

Warily deciding that was the right thing to do with his intended woman barefoot and pregnant in below-teens weather, Michael followed Bailey. She shut the front door, then turned to face him.

"I don't think I ever noticed before how much we argue."

"We don't really—"

She put her hands on her hips. "Do you think we'd get along outside of bed, Michael?"

He tried not to stare at her body through the thin nightgown that outlined her so femininely in the soft glow of a nearby lamp. "Frankly, the fact that we get along so well in bed gives me hope for all the other aspects of our marriage.''

''Does it?'' She raised her eyebrows.

This was tricky territory. No woman wanted to think the man only wanted sex from her. But damn it, the lovemaking between them was wonderful! Wasn't that a good thing? ''I think—*I'm sure* that the couple which sleeps together often is a happy couple,'' he said swiftly, smiling at the clever reply that had come to him.

''I happen to think marriages that are built on great sex burn out once the initial attraction is gone.''

He frowned, confused. ''I'm pretty sure I'm past the initial attraction point with you, Bailey.''

Her face fell. ''You are?''

''Oh, definitely. Initially I just wanted to have sex with you. Now, I just want—'' She was frowning again, and Michael thought he was headed down the wrong path. ''Well, now I'd just rather sit and hold hands with you,'' he said desperately. ''And be a good father and husband,'' he amended quickly, seeing that she seemed close to tears.

''Then we might as well not get married!''

That wasn't the reaction he'd been seeking. ''We have to.''

''Why? Why? We don't have to, Michael. Marriages that don't start out for the right reasons end in divorce.''

''Well, this one's not,'' he said stubbornly. ''I've had all of that divorce stuff I want to in one lifetime with my own parents, and I can tell you it's hard on the children. And everyone else.''

She was obviously uncertain and upset. He pulled

her into his arms, kissing her forehead. "I think you're letting too much get to you at once."

He was surprised when her fingers touched the top button of his shirt. One by one, she undid his buttons.

"Bailey, what are you doing?" Not that he didn't like it, but he wanted to make certain he understood what she wanted from him at this point. No more jumping the gun about that lovemaking stuff. It seemed to aggravate her greatly.

"I want to see if you want to hold my hand. Or anything else."

Now he was starting to feel anxious. Her light fingers had reached the last button she could get to, and she pulled his shirt from his jeans. "I want to hold everything you've got," he managed, his voice ripping from his throat. Didn't she know that what she was doing to him required his last ounce of self-control not to sweep her into his arms and carry her up the stairs to make love—preferably all night long? "But I don't want to upset you. I want you to see how well we can get along without making love."

"I'm going to have to fail the test," she said softly, undoing the button on his fly. "Right now, I want to be reminded how well we get along in bed."

"But I don't want to hurt you," Michael said as Bailey pulled him upstairs. "Suppose we just stick with kissing, maybe some heavy making out?" It would be near impossible to keep that resolution, but he was prepared to give it a manful shot if it meant proving to Bailey that he wasn't just after her body.

"Michael, are you afraid to…touch me?"

He hesitated, glancing swiftly over her luscious curves. "I'm not afraid to touch you. Or to kiss you. But I think everything else should wait a while."

Afraid that her feelings might be getting hurt, he
quickly added, "I mean, the second you mentioned
making love, I could have jumped over the house, but
now that I see your…stomach, I…" His gaze was riv-
eted to where her nightgown softly veiled her rounded
body, which hadn't been so obvious with her blouses
untucked over jeans and sweats. That was a good excuse, wasn't it? Medical conditions were always an
acceptable out. Look at the fence-sitters. They were a
doctor's permit for all occasions. Surely the health
routine would work for him, too. "I'm worried about
your health. And I've been instructed by everyone that
I should be honest about my feelings, so I am."

"I mean to prove to you that I'm perfectly
healthy," she assured him. "Since you're so concerned." She plucked his belt from him.

"I *am* concerned. I don't think you eat enough. Are
you taking those pregnancy vitamins?"

She put her fingers over his lips. "Michael, I'm fine.
If you don't wear me out trying to take care of me,
everything is going to be wonderful. Doc Watson says
I'll probably have a breeze of a pregnancy now that
I'm done with the morning sickness. He said my
mother always had an easy time after that, so I should,
too." She guided him into her room.

He still vacillated. "Well, here, lie down." He motioned her into her bed, sitting on the edge so he could
pull his boots off as he stared at her. "It doesn't even
flatten out when you lay down."

"No." She smoothed a hand over her stomach. "I
think it's too late for flattening."

She frowned when he got in beside her with his shirt
and jeans on. "Michael, what are you doing?"

"Sleeping with you. Isn't that what I'm supposed

to be doing?'' He raised up on an elbow to look at her.

She tugged at his shirt. ''Whether you like it or not, you're going to make love to me.''

''I've got cold feet.''

''Well, leave your socks on, then, but the rest—''

He nuzzled her neck. ''I mean, I've been frothing at the bit for weeks to get inside you,'' he said huskily, ''but I'd rather wait than risk, uh, damaging something.''

''You're not going to!''

''Did Doc Watson say so?''

Bailey was about to lose patience. The feel of Michael next to her, so close but about as pliable as a mule, was more than she could bear. ''No, he didn't say so, but I didn't ask him. I'm sure he would have said it was fine.''

''Why didn't you ask him?''

''I didn't think we'd be making love any time soon!''

''Maybe we shouldn't.''

She straddled him, all her weight purposefully anchoring him. Slapping his hands away, she tugged the buttons through the buttonholes, undid his jeans and jerked down the zipper. ''Off,'' she stated, her tone no-nonsense. ''It's unhealthy to sleep in jeans.''

''Okay, but just listen for a sec, Bailey.'' He shrugged out of his shirt, and she got off him long enough for him to kick off his jeans. ''We'd always regret it if we hurt something. I can wait until you call Doc Watson in the morning and get the green light.''

She kissed his lips, pushing him back on the bed. She nibbled his chin, and he groaned.

''Bailey,'' he whispered. ''I'm trying to take care

of you. But I'm not going to be able to hold out if you're doing things like that.''

He ran his hands under her gown until her hips were in his palms. Bailey watched him close his eyes for a moment. His expression was that of a man who was totally, sublimely happy. And terribly tortured.

But then he looked at her. ''Please, Bailey. There are two of my progeny in there taking up space inside your little belly, and I'd really feel better if we waited until you talk to Doc.''

She rocked a little on his body. It was wonderfully obvious how much he desired her. ''I'd be fine, Michael. I'd tell you if you hurt me.''

He sat up instantly, gently pushing her off him. ''By then it might be too late. There could be brain damage or something.''

She laughed. ''Even you can't get that close to the babies at this stage of the pregnancy.''

''But you don't really know, do you? Do you know anyone who had twins? This is serious.''

He was so upset that Bailey sensed lovemaking was out of the picture. She lay down beside him, putting her head on his chest. It felt good just to lay with him, anyway. ''No, I don't.''

''We've waited this long. It's not going to kill us to wait another day. Well,'' he said sorrowfully, ''it may kill *me*. I doubt I'll be able to ride comfortably tomorrow.''

''We can find other ways to—''

He captured her lips with his, stealing her breath with his passion. ''No, thanks,'' he said huskily, after a long kiss. ''Take your choice, Nevada or a three-day waiting period in Texas. I'm either getting a marriage license in Fallen tomorrow or driving your pretty little self to Nevada. Or I could fly you, if the doctor okays it. You call the doc and ask if it's okay for us to make love, but whether it's in Texas or Nevada, I want to have plenty of steam left to celebrate getting naked with you properly.''

"I'll take the three-day waiting period in Texas.'' Her heart pounded, though, and she wondered if she could wait that long now that she and Michael were headed to the altar.

He frowned. "I don't know if I should give you seventy-two hours to change your mind. I heard women are triply emotional during pregnancy, and I'm here to bear witness to that fact. Of course, it's been an exciting couple of days. Weeks, even. So you should let me rub your back so you can get some rest.''

"You should be making love to me,'' she grumbled, "and you're falling down on the job. You keep thinking up excuses not to.''

He ran a searching hand all the way up her gown, smoothing his rough palm along her side until he reached the soft rise of her breast. Bailey thought she was suffering until he ran his thumb lightly over her nipple. She moaned, feeling the fire light hotter inside her.

"I'm not thinking up excuses not to do anything, Bailey. I want you, both married and otherwise.'' He placed a light kiss on her lips. "Let's do things in the proper order. Doctor and marriage license first. I've got to get your intention to marry me on a legal document.''

"What a hard bargain you drive.''

"The only thing hard around here is your head,'' he retorted.

"I beg to differ." She ran a quick, assessing hand inside his Jockeys.

"Bailey." He said her name on a groan. "I'm going home if you don't play fair."

Kissing his chin, she scooted closer so that they lay touching, her forehead to his chin. Tantalizingly slowly, she removed her hand. "I'll call Doc's office as soon as it opens."

"I'll be by to pick you up at nine. We'll head into town for breakfast and a marriage license. But I'll believe you're mine when I've got the lasso wrapped securely around you, little mama," he murmured, his eyes closing.

Bailey drew a deep, frustrated breath. Somehow Michael had managed to get into her bed without making love to her. That wasn't like him at all. If she was in a bed with him, he was quick to join her in soul-stirring, hungry loving.

She frowned into the darkness. Was Michael past his initial attraction to her? But no. She'd felt his desire for her, as evident and powerful as ever. So he'd put her off for another reason—maybe it *was* the babies.

Which was what she'd been afraid of all along—that he'd marry her just because she was pregnant.

When all she'd ever wanted was for him to love her.

"MR. MICHAEL?"

His eyes popped open at the sound of a small voice at his ear. Jerking the covers up, he stared at the contingent of small Dixons staring curiously at him.

"Whatcha doing in Bailey's bed?" Baby asked.

Next to him, Bailey put her face against his shoulder to hold in what he thought was definitely a snicker.

"I'm uh, uh, ahem…" He searched frantically for an answer. "Making sure your sister wakes up on time to get to work."

"Oh." Baby gazed at him. Her lamb poked at his chin with its cold nose.

"Baby, why don't you take your lamb outside for a while?" Bailey asked. "The rest of you can head down to the breakfast table. I'll be there in a second."

Still staring at Michael, which nearly made him break a sweat, they silently obeyed their sister.

"Well, clearly I overslept my welcome. Sorry about that." He got up and slid into his jeans and boots.

Bailey watched him dress appreciatively. "Soon, they'll be waking you up every morning."

His hands stilled on his shirt buttons. "No way. I'm usually up and gone by now." He sat on the bed, giving her a swift yet urgent kiss. "I'll be back in an hour to pick you up."

"I'll be ready." The smile she gave him was hesitant. "I've got to call Gunner and ask him if I can take the day off."

He paused, not liking that one bit. "Why don't you call him and give your notice?"

She shook her head. "I like working there."

"Not after we're married, though."

"Why not? It's easy money, Michael."

"You don't need money anymore! Brad's on the road to artist stardom, and you're marrying me. You don't need Gunner's money!"

Getting out of bed, Bailey rewarded him with a vision of curves, which showed nicely under the white nightgown as she reached for a robe. "I'm not marrying you for money. So I still need to work."

"Bailey, look," he began, recognizing by her face that this was one argument he was destined to lose but not liking the fact one bit. "I can't have my wife working for Gunner. You'll have plenty to do taking care of the twins, not to mention the other five children who'll be in the house."

"I'm not having twins today, Michael, and I'm not ever going to discuss the Dixon financial situation in any depth with you. That's between Brad and I."

He frowned. "What does that mean?"

"It means that money should never come up where you and I are concerned. I won't need your money." She frowned at him. "Have I not made myself completely clear on this point over the course of our relationship? I will not be marrying you so that I am fiscally cared for."

"No, you are marrying me and so you *will* be fiscally cared for." He gritted out the words between his teeth. "Bailey, that's the dumbest thing I ever heard."

"Separate checking accounts are common in many households, Michael. Welcome to the twenty-first century. Actually, it was this way in the twentieth, but apparently, that information never reached you."

"Wait a minute." He put up his palms to ward off any more words. "I know what you're doing. You're picking a silly fight because you're chickening out. Just like last night, with this you-only-want-me-for-my-body story. Bailey Dixon, in the next seventy-two hours you are becoming Mrs. Bailey Wade, no matter how many smoke screens you invent."

"Oh." She chewed her lip for a second. "I hadn't thought about that."

"About what?" he asked suspiciously.

"Being Mrs. Bailey Wade."

"Who did you think you were going to be?"

"Mrs. Bailey Dixon-Wade?" She jutted her chin at him.

He looked around him. "I'm sorry. I thought you were talking to someone I haven't met. There'll be no Dixon hyphen Wades in my household, Bailey."

"Don't be sarcastic, Michael." Crossing her arms, she said, "I think Dixon-Wade is a lovely last name for the girls. And it will save confusion for the other five kids who will still be Dixons."

"I think you just lost me."

"I'll find you again in an hour." She gave him a push toward the bedroom door. "I've got to fix the children's breakfast and get them loaded up for school."

He allowed himself to be herded down the stairs and out the front door, where Bailey gave him a fast kiss and deserted him on the porch. The door was closed firmly in his face. "Dixon-Wade?" he repeated to himself. "Separate checking accounts?"

Had he missed something? Severely confused, Michael headed to his own house.

BAILEY SWIFTLY DRESSED and went into the kitchen to fix breakfast for her siblings. All six of them sat at the table, patiently waiting, but not for food. Brad had put bowls of cereal at each place, but every gaze was on her.

"The kids say we had an unexpected guest in the house last night," Brad casually mentioned.

She felt her face heat with instant embarrassment. "I had planned to tell you all in a more proper manner, but Michael and I have decided to get married. Not that, of course, we meant to be, um, seen by the children before the fact.''

Her brother laid his spoon down. ''Congratulations! That's great news!''

''A wedding!'' five-year-old Baby exclaimed. ''Will Mr. Michael be our new daddy?''

Bailey and Brad looked at each other in consternation.

''No,'' Bailey said swiftly. ''He'll be an uncle. Right?'' she asked Brad. ''Uncle Michael?''

He shrugged. ''They've got me on that one.''

''Well, we'll work all that out later,'' she said brightly. ''I just wanted to tell you the news.''

Baby clapped her hands. ''We can all take turns sleeping with Mr. Michael! First he can sleep in my bed, and then Amy's, and then Paul's, and then Sam's, and then Beth's, and then he can sleep with Brad.'' She beamed, her little face alight with the idea. ''And then it's your turn again, Bailey.''

''Baby, I'm afraid Michael's not quite like your lamb, honey. We won't share him quite that way, although he will be part of our family,'' Bailey explained. ''He's only going to sleep in my room.''

''I don't think that's fair,'' Amy complained. ''We all like him, too.''

Brad and Bailey glanced at each other, trying to hide smiles. ''I'm sure he'll want to play with all of you often. But when a couple gets married, they sleep in the same bed.'' Bailey felt like she was blushing all over. She kissed each child on the head and hugged her brother. ''Can you handle them so I can get ready to leave with Michael?''

"I believe you fielded all the tough questions. Should be a piece of cake now."

"I want cake," Baby said.

"We'll have wedding cake in three days," Bailey promised. "You'll like that."

"Oh, I can't wait!" Baby and all the children clapped their hands. "Wedding cake and Mr. Michael!"

The children began battling over what games Mr. Michael would play with them, and what toys they would give him to make him feel welcome to their home, and a twinge of unease hit Bailey. They'd discussed checking accounts and hyphenated last names, but in their hurry to start welding their separate lives into one, they forgot a very important question. Where were they going to live? She couldn't leave the children, and yet all of them couldn't move into Michael's house. Brad wouldn't feel comfortable moving over there, but he wouldn't want to be without his sisters and brothers, either. She and Brad had shared parenting duties. It wouldn't feel right to any of them to pull this family apart.

Michael wouldn't want to move into the Dixon house.

Bailey hoped this question wouldn't be as difficult as the other two they'd discussed this morning. One thing was becoming clear. Though she and Michael got along very well in bed, maybe they hadn't developed a deep enough relationship with each other to make a marriage last.

They needed to have a long talk—before they bought the marriage certificate.

Chapter Seventeen

Michael walked into the kitchen, realizing with a sense of relief that the three fence-sitters and his mother were eating breakfast. He was relieved until they started in on him.

"You get lost last night, boss?" Chili asked.

"No." Michael poured a mug of coffee and seated himself. "I believe I got found."

"Yeah?" Everyone perked up at the table.

"Bailey and I are going to get a marriage license today. I've finally talked that stubborn woman into marrying me."

"Oh, Michael. That's wonderful!" His mother leaned over to hug him and kiss him on the cheek.

"We knew you could do it," Chili added. "Just didn't know how long it would take ya."

"You act like I was the one hesitating, but it's Bailey who's been dragging her feet," he protested.

"That's what Chili meant," Curly explained. "We wondered how long it would take you to convince her. We knew you were ripe for the picking when we saw you spying out the kitchen window on her."

Michael grimaced, knowing his mother shared the genial ribbing he was receiving, since they'd both admitted to watching the Dixon family out the kitchen window. He glanced at her, but she smiled warmly.

"I'm going to be an honest grandma," she said. "I can't wait to hold those grandchildren of mine."

"Grandchildren?" Fred sat up. "As in plural?"

Michael nodded, resisting the urge to grin. He was pretty proud of the fact he'd managed twins.

Curly slapped him on the back. "Double trouble for ya."

"Couldn't be happier about it." He scratched his neck before looking around the table at his good luck charms, his conspirators. Burr sticky and slick as he'd resolved to be where Bailey was concerned, asking her to marry him had been the easy part. Dealing with the aftershocks had him a bit buffaloed. "Guess Bailey says she's going to be Mrs. Bailey Dixon-Wade," he said as casually as possible.

Four pairs of eyes stared at him.

"Does that make you Michael Dixon-Wade?" Chili wanted to know.

"Gosh, if anybody's going to buy towels for your wedding present, they better know to monogram them D-W," Curly conjectured.

Michael paused, not liking that. The ranch was the Walking W. Walking D-W just didn't sit right with him. "I don't need any towels."

"Doesn't matter. You'll get all kinds of important junk you never knew you needed for a happy marriage once you announce your nuptials," Fred told him. "That's the fun of having a wedding."

"Doesn't sound like any fun to me." He glared at them. "You're getting me off my point."

"Didja have one, boss?" Chili wanted to know.

"Yes! I wanted to mention this hyphenation problem. I mean, separate checking accounts I could understand. But that other kinda bothered me." He didn't like to admit he'd run into a snag.

"Well," Fred began, his voice sage, "it doesn't matter what she calls herself as long as you get her married to ya."

It was still somehow a blow to his pride. He wanted his wife to be a Wade. But if the grizzled elders and his mother didn't see anything wrong with it, he'd try to live with it.

"Can I give you a small piece of advice, Michael?" his mother asked.

"That's what I'm looking for, small, digestible pieces of advice."

She winked at him. "Tell her how you feel. About anything and everything. Don't keep anything locked up inside you."

The three cowboys nodded in agreement.

"Shoot, I knew that." He had learned *that*. But his pride had reared up and obscured his vision over Bailey's unexpected ideas. "I reckon I just felt like it would be reason for commentary, and we've got enough of that."

"Oh, I guess it doesn't matter what folks say. The only two humans in the marital union are the husband and wife," Cora said. "I'd say Bailey's trying to figure out how she's going to fit you into her life. Remember, Michael, she's juggling more balls in the air than you are. It might be easier if you go along with anything she thinks is best, especially if it's not that bothersome to you. These are the little decisions that make folks fight."

"All right." He blew out a breath. "I'd better go

shower.'' Looking around at all of them, he said, ''Thanks.''

''You just drop in anytime you need sense knocked into your head,'' Fred told him. ''We'll be happy to do it.''

''Don't you belong somewhere else?'' Michael demanded. ''Doesn't somebody else employ you?'' He was half kidding but he made his voice deep and stern since Fred had become a traitor.

Fred shrugged, apparently untroubled by working for one man while continuing to eat at the table of another. ''Grub's better here. Gossip's better over here. There's no action at Gunner's. It's so well run there's nothing hardly for me to do. And there's no trouble getting stirred up.''

''Thanks. That's just what I wanted to hear.'' Michael stomped upstairs, well aware he was being badgered so he had to act grumpy about it. Truth be known, he liked having all of them downstairs for moral support, even if some of them were more fence splitters than sitters.

No need for anyone to know just how nervous he was beginning to feel about tying the knot.

AFTER MICHAEL LEFT the room, the fence-sitters glanced at each other.

''Seen any visions lately, Fred?'' Chili asked.

''I haven't.'' Fred puckered his forehead.

''You musta misunderstood your vision, Fred.'' Curly shook his bald head. ''They didn't say to keep her outta his...I mean—'' he glanced at Cora ''—I mean, maybe they said she'd already been there and so we needed to get those two rounded up toward the altar.''

"They did say Bailey was fixing to have a life-altering event, and that it would be hard to get her to marry Michael," Fred said slowly.

Chili pulled at his bushy white mustache. "That'd be finding out she was having twins."

"Heck, no. It was becoming a millionaire." Curly grinned.

"She's not really a millionaire by the time all the taxes are levied and paid. I say it was having Deenie Day announce her predicament to all of Fallen." Fred scratched at his chin. "Of course, all of these things together are enough to make a body feel like they're inhabiting a whirlwind."

"Either way, it appears that there's still some trouble up ahead." Chili gulped some coffee for fortification.

"Excuse me," Cora said gently. "It seems to me that we should just leave Michael and Bailey to do what comes naturally in their relationship at this point. They're getting married. I know you three mean well, but don't you think Michael and Bailey are on a smooth road now?"

The three cowboys slowly shook their heads. Always the leader, Chili spoke up. "Ma'am, with all due respect, this has been a near-impossible line to draw between two contrary points. We'll not breathe an easy breath until we hear, 'I now pronounce you husband and wife!'"

"I DON'T REALLY want to do this," Bailey protested. "Let's just get a plain gold band and be done with it."

Michael stared around the room at the array of glass jewelry cases before squeezing her hand. "You've had your say about last names and separate checking, Bailey. Either you choose a diamond or I do, but we're leaving here with something for my bride.''

She knew he meant it. Such expense for a token of affection didn't seem right, particularly when she wasn't completely certain of Michael's motivation for affection. With the whole town knowing she was an unwed mother, anything more than a plain band seemed to further announce that she'd caught herself a wealthy man by getting pregnant.

''Michael, Bailey. How are you?'' An elderly man came forward, his eyes twinkling. ''I was wondering when you two would be getting around to see me.''

''Good morning, Mr. Dawson,'' Michael said cheerily to the store owner.

Bailey thought she blushed from the toes of her boots to the top of her hair. Mr. Dawson and anyone else who saw them in the jewelry store would know why they were here. After Deenie's big announcement, there wasn't a citizen in Fallen who didn't know of her plight.

Michael glanced at Bailey. ''We're looking for an engagement ring, if you've got any to show us.''

''That I do,'' Mr. Dawson said cheerily. ''And may I offer my congratulations?'' He began unlocking some cases. ''Although I'm not surprised to hear you're finally marrying.''

Bailey felt like she was frozen in place with embarrassment. There was no way she could go through with this, not in this small town where everyone had known her since she began crawling. *I should have made Michael take me into Dallas,* she thought wildly.

But it was too late for that because Mr. Dawson laughed and gestured to the two cases he'd unlocked.

"Now, the ordinary rule of thumb is to spend about two month's salary for a diamond." He winked at Bailey.

"By that standard then, we'll take a look at some of these." Michael pointed into a tray that held tiny chip diamonds teenagers might give each other. He glanced innocently at Bailey. "The beef industry has been way down for the last two months."

She stared at him, unable to say a word. All she could think about suddenly was the water rights she'd offered to Gunner.

"Oh, come on, Bailey. I'm kidding."

"My mother never had a diamond," she murmured, wanting desperately to talk Michael out of spending money.

"Then I owe it to her daughter to make certain *she* does. This is real hard on Bailey," Michael explained to the jeweler.

"I see it is. Well, Bailey's always been a modest girl. You know, we have some that come in and the first words out of their mouth are, 'I want to see the biggest ring you've got.'"

"I want to see the biggest ring you've got," Michael immediately responded.

Bailey's painful humiliation increased. "Michael!"

"I've got a five-carat diamond, and a ten-carat, both of excellent quality," Mr. Dawson assured them.

"I don't want anything like that!" Bailey was adamant. It wasn't her style. What would she do, wear a diamond larger than her fingernail to chase sheep and children?

"I tell you what, Bailey," Michael said. "How about if I choose three rings, and you select the one of the three that appeals to you most?"

"Thank you," she said miserably. She wasn't about to stare down into the cases at all the sparkling things. She didn't own a necklace or a bracelet. A watch and her mother's thin wedding band were all she had. She went and sat in a chair by Mr. Dawson's desk while the men went over the trays.

She understood this was important to Michael. Unfortunately, he didn't understand that she wasn't marrying him for money, or for any other aspiration. She loved him. She desperately wanted him to love her in return, not feel responsible for her. There were so many things about him that she had always loved—the way he looked, long and slim, in blue jeans, the wonderful care of his ranch and home, his treatment of his employees, and lately, the kind way in which he endured her family. Bailey sighed and stared out the window. She'd lost hope that he would ever love her, and that had fueled her to make a decision she regretted now. But it was too late. She couldn't go back on the contract with Gunner.

"Okay." Michael came over to her with three velvet boxes. Mr. Dawson respectfully remained on the opposite side of the room as Michael hunkered at Bailey's feet. "These are what I like. You may not like any of them. If you don't prefer any of these, I'll try again. I want you to be happy, Bailey."

"Diamonds aren't exactly what I need to be happy." She stared at his strong face, his deep blue eyes and well-cut black hair. "You don't have to do this."

"I do. I want Gunner to know you're spoken for, and spoken for loudly."

He winked at Bailey, but she couldn't laugh. "Is

that why you're doing this?'' she whispered urgently. Were they back to the old rivalry?

"Hell, no,'' he whispered back. ''I know the Dixon household is a family of artists, and they can be kind of nontraditional and flaky, but I'm a real stickler for tradition myself. I've been on the same ranch all my life except for college and a few vacations. It's the same ranch my father built, and I'm about as unchanging as the black soil my house was built on. My children will grow up in that house, and my wife will live there with me, whether she hyphenates or banks at a different bank.''

"I've been meaning to talk to you about those subjects.'' Bailey wouldn't have chosen Mr. Dawson's jewelry store to discuss this, but since Michael had brought it up, maybe this was the best time. Gazing at him earnestly, she said, ''I was wondering if we could live in my house.''

"Your house?'' Michael frowned. That hadn't exactly been a thought he'd entertained. Why would she want to remain in the dilapidated Victorian? ''Is it because of my mother?''

"Oh, no,'' Bailey quickly assured him. ''I like Cora. She reminds me of my mother. I've enjoyed having her to talk to.''

He rocked back on his heels, still holding the three unopened velvet boxes. ''I didn't expect you'd prefer to live in your house. Mine is bigger.''

"But it's just the children…'' Her words filtered away while she stared at him with huge eyes. ''Michael, do you ever stop and think about exactly what it is you're taking on with me? Five small children—''

"Five small children, four more months of pregnancy, three nosy cowboys, two newborn rug rats and a lamb under an oak tree. I know, Bailey. It's a common refrain I've run through my mind. It's scary, I'll admit, but you should run all the more quickly to catch me because I'm man enough to take it all on.''

For the first time this morning, Bailey smiled at him. Michael was greatly relieved. ''Okay?''

''Okay.''

''Start running, then. We'll talk about where we going to shack up later.'' He held up the boxes. ''Future Mrs. Dixon-Wade, I can't marry you until you eeny-meeny-miny-mo.''

''I wish you'd be serious about this!'' Bailey's voice was filled with laughter, and her lips softened a bit in spite of her stern words, so Michael knew he was finally wearing her somberness away.

''Here's what's behind curtain number one.'' He opened the first box to reveal a sparkling pear-shaped diamond with baguettes on either side.

''Oh, it's lovely,'' Bailey said approvingly, instantly reaching to snatch the ring from its box to try on.

''Now you're acting more like a girl,'' he teased.

She gave him a jaundiced stare. ''It's still pretty big.''

''You can use it as a flashlight if you get lost at night.'' He opened the second box to reveal an emerald-cut diamond set in gold.

''Oh, that's lovely, too!'' Bailey reached for the ring and tried it on another finger.

''Did I mention you can only have one?''

''Mmm.'' She moved her hands to catch the light in the diamonds. ''Let me see the tiebreaker.''

He laughed and snapped the box open, glad that she was finally enjoying herself. Inside, a large oval diamond glimmered in platinum, stunning in its simplicity.

"Oh, my gosh," she whispered, pulling the other two off her fingers and handing them to Michael. "I'll take the tiebreaker."

"It's my favorite, too." He handed the others to Mr. Dawson, who had come to surreptitiously stand beside them as the final selection was reviewed. "She was able to make up her mind."

"It looks beautiful on you, Bailey." Mr. Dawson's grin was huge.

"Well, all that's left is the pain of paying the bill," Michael couldn't resist saying just to see Bailey grimace. He kind of liked getting under unflappable Bailey's skin.

"Oh, no, we're not finished yet," she said, surprising him with the determination in her voice.

"You really can only have one, honey."

"Yes, but you need a wedding ring." She stood, still wearing the oval and not about to part with it. "I think it's only fair that you wear something that says you're spoken for loudly, as well."

"Uh—I can't wear a wedding ring," Michael protested, not about to give in any easier than she had. "I heard it's dangerous to wear those things. I could get it caught in a fence."

"Hard to catch it on a split-rail fence. Bring the tray, please, Mr. Dawson. I think platinum, to go with my ring." Her smile was knowing as she was left with Michael. "Don't even try to wiggle out of this."

"It might cut off my circulation!"

Bailey laughed at him. "I intend to keep your circulation moving quite briskly, thank you very much."

"I'll hold you to that promise."

They quickly selected a set of matching bands, paid Mr. Dawson and left the store. Once on the pavement, in the bright sunlight, Bailey stared at her new engagement ring. "Michael, I think this is the most beautiful ring I've ever seen. Thank you so much."

"Well." His throat was clogged with emotion. "I think you're the most beautiful woman I've ever laid eyes on."

They stared at each other. Michael had never wanted to grab her, drive her swiftly home and make urgent love to her so badly. "I'm glad you finally roped me," he said gruffly.

"Oh, right. Who was holding the end of that lasso?" she retorted as they walked toward his car.

He held her to him as they walked, thinking she had held the lasso and caught him, but it was better for her to think it was the other way around.

"I know exactly what you're thinking," she told him, patting him very patronizingly on the butt. "Don't kid yourself."

"Man, if this is what marriage is all about, what have I gotten myself into?" He swept Bailey up in his arms, stopping to kiss her right on the mouth in the middle of the street.

"Michael!" she protested.

"I'd like to carry you right home and put you in my bed."

"My bed."

"We've still got to iron that out." He moved as a truck rumbled down the street, but he still stared at Bailey. "My mother says I should do whatever you think is best."

"I like Cora so much. I hope she likes me."

The two got along well. For some reason, that made

him awfully happy. "She does. Back to the living arrangements."

"I think at least in the beginning it might be easier on the children if they stay in their own house," Bailey admitted.

"What about Brad? He's not going to want to move all his artist stuff over to my house permanently. He isn't going to want to leave his house, but he's not going to want the kids gone, either."

"No," Bailey murmured.

"He's not going to want to be awakened at night by yelling babies who want their mother, though," he said with a glint of mischief in his eye.

"Their father, you mean!" She tapped him on the chin. "I bet you can warm a bottle just as easy as you do your coffee."

"Yeah, but then there's the thorny issue of changing diapers."

"Thorny? Do you mean fragrant?"

He ignored that. "And while we're on the subject of thorny issues and putting our two households together, I think you could have mentioned that you were selling the water rights to your property to Gunner."

She stared at him, her eyes worried. "We do have a lot of things to work out. We need to talk about taking some marriage classes, not to mention where we're going to be married and—" Her thoughts trailed away and back to the main division between them. "Michael, I can't change the water rights contract now."

"I know. It's okay. I can have my own pond dug for my cattle, Bailey, but in the future, let's work together instead of against each other." He set her down and unlocked his car door. She remained at his side, her head bowed, her expression upset. He didn't want her being upset on a day that was supposed to be one of the happiest in their lives. So far, everything between them could be worked out with a little patience and understanding. "Hey," he said, "don't look now, but the Rodeo Queen is watching our every move."

"If I flash my diamond, it'll blind her."

"Maybe turn her into a pillar of salt."

"That only happens if she sees you kissing me."

Instantly, he swept her into a soul-stealing kiss. After a few seconds, he forgot about Deenie and everything else in the town square except how holding Bailey made him feel whole.

"Did it work?" Bailey asked a moment later, when they pulled apart long enough for air.

"Oh, it worked, lady. It always works just fine. I've got to sit down now before all of Fallen knows just how well it works. But Deenie wasn't really around. It was a great way to sneak a kiss out of you, not that you're jealous of her or anything."

"I'm not!"

He laughed and helped Bailey into the car, glad it had been so easy to change the subject. Just thinking about Gunner and his girl had suddenly made his gut clench painfully. Gunner had even offered to marry Bailey, as if Michael wasn't capable of taking care of his own woman.

Anger and male pride surged through him. He tried to tamp it down, but Bailey had done the one thing he wished she hadn't—given Gunner the upper hand over him.

FROM THE WINDOW of her daddy's store, Deenie *did* see Michael and Bailey entering the courthouse, or else she might not have known until Fallen gossip reached her that something important was in the air. Since there was a pregnancy involved, the logical assumption was that there was finally going to be a wedding, a hunch that was confirmed when she later spied them hurrying into Mr. Dawson's jewelry store. She figured the wedding would be small, since there was a matter of haste involved.

All the better, as far as Deenie was concerned. She'd have a better chance of catching Brad once his sister moved over to Michael's. There was no question in her mind that she had to have the artist. He might have made her a little famous—and her daddy a lot of money—but she wanted Brad. And he wanted her—very badly. There was just that little problem of him being angry with her over what she'd done to Bailey.

Ingratiating herself with the bride was a sensational idea. What Bailey Dixon needed was a full-blown, down-home, more-is-always-better shower given in her honor. This would allow Deenie to get closer to Brad and impress him with the depth of her sincere repentance. It might also earn her forgiveness from the bride-to-be, very necessary for gaining entrée into the close-knit Dixon family.

Deenie chewed on a long nail, deep in thought, when Michael and Bailey hurried from the jewelry store. She smiled to herself. A party would definitely liven things up for the happy couple.

The question was, lingerie or baby shower surprise?

Chapter Eighteen

"A do-drop-in combination bridal-baby shower in honor of Bailey Dixon and Michael Wade!" Chili glanced up from the town newspaper. "Hosted by Deenie Day."

"You've got to be kidding me." Fred hurried over to read the black-and-white half-page invitation. "Everyone come celebrate this joyous occasion!" he read in astonishment.

"Bailey and Michael didn't mention this." Curly frowned, his peppered brows bushy under his pate.

"You don't suppose..." Chili stared at his compatriots.

They all jumped to their feet and hurried up the hill to the ranch house. Michael sat at the table eating lunch with Cora. "Excuse us for bursting in here," Chili said, "but did you know you were having a party tonight?"

They both frowned at him.

"What party?" Michael asked.

The three cowboys somberly removed their hats from their heads. "A do-drop-in combination bridal-baby shower, complete with barbecue, chilled strawberry pie and refreshments, given by Deenie Day. The invitation is right there on the front page of the newspaper, big as life and twice as ugly," Chili intoned. He cleared his throat. "I hope you're planning on telling Bailey, because we don't want to be the messengers who get shot!"

MICHAEL STARED in horror at the scrolling letters of the invitation. Trust Deenie to find a way to make even an ugly newspaper invitation look elegant.

Bailey was going to scream.

As it was, he had barely managed to get an engagement ring on her finger. She didn't want anybody giving her anything! And this would feel so much like charity to her. Bailey had always been especially prickly about handouts.

"This is very bad." His insides felt like the sandwich he'd just eaten wasn't going to digest.

"Wonder what Deenie was thinking?" Cora asked.

"How to get Brad to forgive her, I'd guess." He folded the newspaper and stood. "I'm going over to Bailey's. If you hear screams, it's just me getting my head chewed off."

Shoulders slumped, he went out the back door. The three cowboys and Cora sighed. "I hope Bailey is satisfied with his head and doesn't decide to have Deenie's head for dessert."

"WHAT?" Bailey snatched the newspaper from Michael, staring at the black-on-white words in horror. "How could she?" Desperately, she glanced at Michael. "There's got to be a way to stop this. Call the *Gazette* office and have them stop deliveries. Buy every copy on the streets. Do something!"

"Honey." He reached to pull her into his arms. "It's too late. Maybe nobody will see it."

"Everybody will see it! How embarrassing!" She burst into tears.

"I'm thinking she meant well."

"I think she still wants you! She's trying to impress you."

He shook his head, at her, his smile wry. "She's trying to impress your brother."

She frowned. "What do you mean?"

"You haven't noticed Brad moping a little ever since the incident at the auction?"

"Well, he's been quiet…" She'd been so caught up in her own never-ending circle of problems, she hadn't focused much on Brad. Now that she thought about it, her brother had been very silent for a man who'd just made a million dollars.

Deenie had humiliated Bailey in front of the town. Brad would never have anything to do with Deenie again—unless Bailey wasn't upset with the Rodeo Queen. Brad was that loyal. "I think I see where you're going with this. I knew Brad fancied Deenie. I just didn't know the feelings were mutual."

Michael shrugged. "I'm only suggesting this might be Deenie's way of cozying up to Brad through you. It's Deenie's way of operating. She always bears gifts of some sort when she wants something."

"Like those darn pies. Brad loves her silly pies. Strawberry just happens to be his favorite."

"I'm suggesting to you that Deenie knows very well what his favorite is. She is an expert at employing the most useful weapons of manipulation."

Bailey sighed. "I don't think I can bear having her

for a sister-in-law. I know that's mean, but she's caused me a lot of pain.''

He pulled her into his arms. ''Try to think of it as a lot of good she caused you with her stupid stunt at the auction. You and I would still be running around butting heads.''

''We still butt heads.'' But Bailey smiled as she relaxed against Michael's hard body.

''There's other parts of you I'd like to tangle with,'' he murmured against her ear.

''Tonight it looks like you'll be receiving a lot of tea towels and rosebud vases. Maybe nobody will come,'' she said hopefully.

''I have a funny feeling, Bailey Dixon soon to be Wade, that folks have been wanting to do something for you and your family for so long that they're going to jump at the chance to attend this hoedown. And the best part about it is it's a casual affair, the weather's just right, and Deenie's paying for it.''

''Michael!'' She turned in his arms, laughing. He caught her lips in a searching kiss, which heated instantly to searing. His hands moved from her shoulders, down her sides and over her bottom. Bailey was certain every pore in her body was electrified by his touch. ''Michael,'' she murmured.

''I'm just hoping somebody gives me one of those garter things.'' He ran a hand under her dress until he reached the top of her thigh, stroking gently. ''If they don't, I'm going to buy one myself.''

''What would you do with it?''

''Take it off of you.'' He bent to press a kiss at the top of each thigh. ''After our wedding, I'm going to kiss every inch of you. Slowly. I have my own favorite kind of dessert.''

Bailey's heart beat like a hummingbird's. She pulled him up to where she look into his eyes. "I can't help being uneasy about this shower, Michael. I wanted everything to be as private and inconspicuous as possible."

"Don't be. Your siblings will have a ball, and everything will be just fine." Of course, he knew what Bailey was thinking, but it was his job to comfort her. Anytime Deenie Day was on a mission, very little good could be expected to come of it.

THE EVENING of the shower favored the bride and groom with twilight skies and warmer weather than they'd been having. Not a cloud in sight, though, perhaps selfishly, Bailey had hoped for rain. But what Deenie wanted she usually got. She was in her element supervising the setup of metal tables and awnings on the Wades' wide front lawn.

There was nothing she could do but be a good sport and attend. Bailey sighed, walking over to the mirror. Her stomach protruded, even in her mother's dress. Possibly she should have bought a new one, but until the inheritance taxes and income taxes were paid— how much did one have to pay to the government when one painting fetched so much money?—she wasn't going to spend anything she didn't have to. And when all the taxes were paid, she was going to buy the children and Brad clothes. With her figure changing so rapidly, there was no reason to buy anything, anyway.

Still, Bailey couldn't help being distressed over how much her stomach protruded. And the lovely two-carat engagement ring flashed like crystal fire on her finger. She looked like a woman who had to get married.

"Ready?"

Bailey turned at Michael's voice.

"Ready to go face the crowd and open presents?" He rubbed his palms briskly together, as if he were greedy.

She couldn't help smiling at him. "I'm sure you're just thrilled to be getting baby supplies and other odds and ends."

He walked forward and wrapped her in his arms. "I am. I am totally thrilled not to have to pay for them myself."

She laughed at the teasing note in his voice, laying her head against his chest.

"I am even more excited that we'll be getting stuff we need. Bailey, I don't have the first clue what babies require. Think of it this way. All the old folks who'll be here tonight have had kids. They know what works and what they wish they'd had in their child-raising years. I consider tonight a bonanza of wisdom and assistance." He moved her chin so he could look into her eyes. "It's not wrong to accept what these people want to give you, honey. Do them a big favor and be happy."

"If it wasn't coming from Deenie, I'd be happier."

He chuckled. "I know. But isn't there some wise saying about not looking a gift horse in the mouth?"

Smiling, she stepped away from his arms to run a hungry gaze over him. "You look handsome."

"I am handsome."

Wryly, she said, "And bragging, too." But there was no denying that Michael Wade was an eyeful and then some. Her heart fluttered as she took in the black Western-cut shirt covering his wide chest, the black belt encircling his flat stomach and the dress blue jeans, which seemed to go on forever in length. Black and gray ostrich-skin boots completed his outfit. She swallowed. "Maybe you have some reason to brag."

"I do. I've got plenty of reason to brag on you. Have I ever told you how beautiful you are?"

"Not with my clothes on." She gave him a winsome stare.

"Oh." He turned serious. "You look beautiful," he said, his voice husky as he ran one hand lingeringly along her arm. "You are beautiful, Bailey."

She couldn't possibly be beautiful with all this stomach waddling in front of her. Michael was just being kind. Looking away, she had a split-second to notice guests were starting to arrive before Michael pulled her into his arms. "I'm not going to look these gift horses in the mouth," he told her, possessively running a hand over her stomach. "They're giving me you."

"Oh, Michael," Bailey whispered. "You really feel that way, don't you?"

"Have you ever known me to say something I didn't?"

She tried to think but it was hard with Michael holding her so close. Honesty was a basic part of his personality she deeply admired. "Maybe just to the cowboys," she teased.

"Well, they deserve it," he said gruffly. "They're scoundrels and live off of me like fleas."

She laughed out loud. "You love them."

"I consider them family. You, I love." He kissed her, long and slow, dizzying Bailey's brain. "See?" he said after a moment, "I'm very happy that they got us together. I know when to accept help when I need it. Now, let's go accept some more help."

Bailey's insides pitched. In spite of all of Michael's words, she was still nervous about tonight. Her heart told her that Michael was right, but she was pregnant and unwed, and it just wasn't something her parents would have been celebrating.

ON THE PORCH, Deenie came to her with a smile. "The guests are starting to arrive. Let me put this corsage on you." Two red roses with baby's breath and greenery were shaped into a lovely decoration, which Deenie unerringly attached to Bailey's dress. "Now, don't you look nice?"

Bailey stared at the flowers, thinking that they rather resembled a scarlet flag right over her blossoming stomach. "Thank you, Deenie."

"Bailey," Deenie said with a nervous glance at Michael standing beside the bride-to-be, "I'm terribly sorry for what I did the other night. I hope you can forgive me."

Her insides shrank. She really didn't want Deenie being nice to her. Bailey couldn't honestly say that she and the Rodeo Queen would ever be friends. "Deenie, I have to ask you, are you doing this because of Brad?"

"Partly," Deenie admitted. "I am dreadfully sorry for what I did, Bailey. I've never had people laugh at me before—at least not right to my face. Maybe they've laughed behind my back. But all that laughter when I've heard only applause all my life—" She sighed, raising her brows as she shook her head slightly. "Bailey, nothing can excuse my behavior."

"Apology accepted. Let's not think about it anymore." Bailey's stomach was starting to pitch uncomfortably.

"Laughter was one of the reasons I would never give Brad the time of day," Deenie said quietly. "I've always kind of thought he was handsome, even sexy. But then I would think, 'Deenie, everybody will laugh if you take up with a starving artist.' I mean, people expect that I'll marry a man who can afford me."

Her helmet hairdo sprayed into place, her lipstick shiny and well-drawn, her makeup complementing her beautiful dress, Deenie Day looked like a doll who'd had the best designers. Only her eyes showed how miserable she was.

Bailey felt herself softening. "There's not going to be much left of the money after we pay inheritance and income taxes," she warned. "We've got five siblings we're raising. Brad and I are never going to have wheelbarrows full of money."

Deenie shook her head. "Once Brad wouldn't have anything to do with me, I realized how much it was going to hurt to lose him. It wasn't a matter of money or status to me after that." Deenie stared at her. "Bailey, he's the only man who's ever loved me in spite of myself. Despite all my flaws, he still sees beauty," she whispered.

Bailey was astonished. Her heart went out to Deenie. "Maybe because of them," she told the suffering woman. "Love has that power."

Deenie looked nervously at Michael. Bailey imagined how difficult it must be for her to bare herself in this way. "I admire your courage, Deenie," she said softly. "Not many people can face the mirror without flinching."

"Oh, I flinch." Deenie glanced at her feet, ashamed. "It's just past time to do something about it."

How could she not completely identify with every word Deenie spoke? Her heart was wringing with compassion and empathy. Bailey took her by the arm so they could walk down the porch together. "Come on. Let's go enjoy this wonderful shower you're throwing."

Michael took Bailey's other hand, squeezing it lightly. She glanced at him and saw the pride in his eyes. Warmth stole over her, and Bailey thought the temperature could drop twenty degrees, and she'd still feel just right.

BAILEY COULDN'T REMEMBER that babies required so many things! She and Michael opened boxes containing strollers, carriers, bibs, diapers, clothes, pacifiers, bottle warmers, swings, diaper-wipe warmers…the list went on and on. "I'm not sure my brothers and sisters had the luxury of any of this," she said in a laughing aside to Michael.

"I'm getting more uneasy by the moment."

"You'll be a great father," she assured him.

"No, I mean I'm going to have to figure out how all of this stuff works. What's that saucer thing on wheels good for, anyway? If Boy One or Boy Two decides to take a walk on the moon?"

She smiled, gazing around at all the presents stacked at their feet. Guests kept arriving, carrying pastel-wrapped boxes. Deenie was a wonderful hostess, greeting each and every person before leading them over to Michael and Bailey. Cora sat to their left, accounting for each guest and their gift in a sweet baby shower book Deenie had given them. Bailey sighed with happiness. "You know, I think I'm actually enjoying this."

Cora patted her on the shoulder. "You ought to."

Bailey squeezed her fingers. "Thanks, Cora." She smiled at Michael's mother. "I'm so glad you decided to stay."

Brightness instantly shone in Cora's eyes. "Don't make me get all sentimental, Bailey. It's more than I ever expected to be at the Walking W at all, much less be enjoying a bridal shower with my son and his lovely wife-to-be. I don't think anybody here tonight is happier than me!"

Curly, Chili and Fred had the hardest tasks of the evening. They took turns supervising the five Dixon children. The boys got to throw the paper and bows in the trash, while the girls carefully carried the presents to the long tables to display. Baby was very little help, though she wanted to be. Both she and her lamb wore discarded bows, the lamb's around its neck and Baby's in her hair.

It made Bailey a bit sad. "I wish my folks were here."

Fred paused as he stooped to pick up the latest present she'd unwrapped. "I'll bet they are, Miss Bailey," he said. "And I bet they're real proud of you."

"Oh, Fred." She smiled at him. "You're a friend to say so."

"Nope. Just right, as usual."

He went on with his duties, and Bailey caught Michael's resigned grin. "You do love them."

"They're family," he argued. "I endure them."

Cora leaned to peer past Bailey. "You'd best be careful. I just might marry one of those fine bachelors."

The smile slid right off Michael's face. "You wouldn't!"

Her laughter was mischievous. "Three handsome men at the Walking W, just begging to be tied down by a woman's loving fingertips. It happened to you—why not one of them?"

"I don't know. The thought just gives me the willies, for some reason."

Bailey gave him a small, playful push on the arm. "None of them seems to be too excited about becoming your stepfather. They'd probably be jumping into line to marry Cora if it wasn't for you."

"I don't want to talk about this," Michael said, his eyes worried.

"We're just picking at you, Michael," Bailey assured him. "You've been way too happy all night."

Cora smiled at him. "I'm just testing that theory you've got about family being something to endure."

"Well, don't test my endurance any further," he said with a groan. "Those three meddle enough without them being related to me by marriage!"

Bailey patted his back as she rose. "I've got to take a lady's break." After talking to about a hundred guests, she'd drunk a lot of punch and needed to freshen up. "I'll be back in a moment, Cora."

"I'll walk you up to the house," Michael told her, rising.

"No, you sit here with Cora and talk to our guests. I'll be right back." Bailey gently pushed him down in his lawn chair and headed to the house. It would be good for folks to see Michael and his mother getting along so well. No doubt much gossip had been stirred up over Cora's unexpected return to Fallen. But the past needed to stay that way, and tonight was a wonderful time to lay ugly gossip to rest. She was waylaid only once or twice to talk before managing to make it to the safety of her home.

"I think it's big of Deenie to do this for poor Bailey," a woman's voice said as Bailey neared the kitchen.

She halted, unseen, in her tracks.

"Well, you know Deenie's madly in love with Michael. Always was. Would have caught him, too, if someone else hadn't figured out a faster way to catch him," another voice replied. "I guess a man gets caught the fastest by a naked woman."

"A naked, pregnant woman."

"I heard Deenie was in love with Brad," a third voice offered.

"Well, *now*. What choice did she have? Michael was taken. And there aren't that many bachelors in Fallen worth a hoot. Brad and Deenie will make a great couple unless…"

The strident voice faltered. Bailey put her hand over her thundering heart, waiting for the next words as breathlessly as the women in the kitchen.

"Unless Bailey somehow gets in the way of that, too."

"I've known Bailey since she was in diapers. I don't think she's got a mean bone in her body," someone protested. "She'd just want Brad to be happy."

"Not happy splitting Brad's million plus with Deenie."

"Ah!" all the gossips exclaimed in unison.

"And then there's the matter of the pregnancy. I see a ring on Bailey's finger, but are they getting married or not? Where's the invitations, I'd like to know? If I'm bringing a gift, shouldn't I be invited to a wedding?"

"I heard he wouldn't marry her."

"I heard she wouldn't marry *him*."

"I heard she was pregnant by Gunner King. Is he here tonight?"

"I saw Gunner out last night with that Yankee girl who's new to town. They looked pretty tight. They might stay that way, unless Bailey decides one man isn't enough for her. 'Course, by the time Bailey bankrupts Michael—and she will, mark my words, with that passel of unruly children. Brad's sure got no head for business, and by the time that million gets sucked up by Uncle Sam and then they blow the rest, I say Miss Bailey's got herself into a pretty fix with Michael. She's going to end up being the financial noose around his neck. Gunner'll end up having to ride in and save the day once more, just like his father did. Everyone knows Polly Dixon got more than one loan from Sherman King when the odd emergency cropped up at the Dixons. Remember the time little Sam broke his arm?"

There was a chorus of yeses.

"There was no health insurance. It was King insurance to the rescue."

"Oh?" the gossips exclaimed. "Tell us more!"

Bailey's face flamed. She didn't want to believe anything she'd heard, but it all sounded so likely, she had a hard time not believing. And if Sherman King had bailed Polly out on occasion, then Gunner was doing no more than his father would have by buying the Dixon water rights.

Only this time, Michael would be hurt.

And nobody, maybe not even she herself, would believe that was the last thing she'd intended to do. Bailey ran upstairs and locked herself in her bedroom.

Throwing herself on the bed, she gave in to her breaking heart.

WHEN BAILEY hadn't returned in twenty minutes, Michael became worried. He stood outside her bedroom, the locked door worrying him even more. "Bailey, let me in."

No one answered him. "Honey, I've practically got paper cuts from all the bows I've had to break on purpose so we'd have lots of kids. I need you to kiss my ouchies." She always hurried to take care of the cowboys' ouchies. Maybe it would work for him as well.

The door stayed shut.

"Bailey," he said urgently, "either you open this door, or I'm coming through it."

The lock unlatched and the door opened an inch. He pushed through, closing it behind him and locking it. "What happened to you? Bailey!"

He pulled her into his arms, seeing at once that she'd been crying. His action made her start weeping all over again. "Stop crying, honey. What's wrong?"

"They're saying awful things," she wept against his chest. "Terrible things, Michael!"

"Who is?"

"The women in the kitchen. They said—they said—"

He tried to get her to look at him but she wouldn't. "What? What did they say?"

A knock softly sounded at the door. "Bailey, it's me," Cora said quietly.

Bailey reached immediately for the door, though Michael might not have done so quite that readily. His mother slipped inside, and he locked the door behind her.

"Oh, Bailey." Cora put out her arms. "I had a funny feeling something had gone wrong. What happened?"

The two women sat on the bed together. Michael was astonished to see Bailey completely turn to his mother with grateful need.

"I heard those women saying that my babies are Gunner's! That Michael won't marry me. That I won't marry Michael. That Deenie really is in love with Michael, but that I stole him from her. And that he has to marry me because I'm pregnant!" Bailey's breath came in small hiccups. "And that I'm going to bankrupt him," she whispered, torn.

Cora held her tightly. "You know none of that is true, Bailey. Every small town has their share of ill-meaning witches. Most everyone here tonight wishes you well." She caught Bailey's face to look at her. "And you know I do."

"Oh, Cora," Bailey said, her voice shaky. "I wanted to avoid this so badly. I always dreamed of having a loving marriage like my folks had. But in a way those women were right. Michael and I have done everything wrong."

Anger flowed through Michael so mightily he felt ten feet tall with emotion. Seeing Bailey in this much pain broke his heart in two and dashed the pieces. He'd do everything in his power if she'd never be so upset again. "You said I needed to say exactly how I feel, Mother, and right now I say enough is enough. I don't care what some town biddies think. I've had all the party I can stand. Bailey, get your wedding dress and pack some clothes. We're driving to Nevada tonight, just me and you and our marriage license.''

Hope flared in Bailey's eyes at his words. She hesitated. "I don't have a wedding dress, Michael.''

"No…wedding dress? We planned on getting married tomorrow night, right? You *were* going to marry me? Are you going to marry me?''

"Of course!'' She jumped to her feet, reaching to hold him in her arms. "If that's what you really want.''

"I want you right now, damn it. Yesterday. Why don't you have a dress?'' He glowered at her, his pride smarting. Most women spent days agonizing over the right gown!

"I just haven't had time to shop,'' Bailey told him. "No, that's not quite true. I'm sorry.'' She looked at him shyly, apologetically. "I guess I was afraid you'd change your mind.''

"I told you I love you, Bailey. I'm waiting to hear the same from you. Are you in love with me or not?''

"Oh, Michael,'' she said huskily, "I have been in love with you forever, I think. I've been so afraid…of you not wanting to marry me, of feeling like I was an obligation….'' Her voice trailed off as she stared into his eyes.

"Bailey Dixon, we're going to do this thing together. We're going to be married, and we're going to spend all our days together. I'm going to watch your pretty hair turn silver, and you're going to watch me get gimpy. And we're going to raise our family together.'' He enfolded her in his arms. "I love you so much, more than I ever thought I could love anyone. But the babies—'' he drew in a deep breath

"—they're just a little more of you to love, baby. And I couldn't be happier about that."

Cora cleared her throat. "Perhaps I can help," she said, getting to her feet. "I haven't given Bailey my present yet."

She pulled Bailey's closet open to reveal a long, elegant candlelight wedding gown. A shoulder-length veil, its headband encrusted with diamanté, hung beside it.

"Oh, Cora! It's beautiful!" Bailey flew to her, throwing her arms around her neck.

"I hope you won't mind me selecting a gown, Bailey. I just had a funny feeling you might not want to do it alone."

Bailey cried all the harder. "Thank you, Cora."

"I just did what your mother would have done if she were here, hon. I kind of thought Polly would approve of my selection."

"Oh, I know she would." Bailey wiped her nose on a tissue Michael handed her. The past was truly laid to rest once and for all. For all the awful whispers that Michael Wade, Senior, had been in love with his neighbor's wife, Bailey knew that none of them had been true. "I'm so glad you're home for good now, Cora. I'm going to need you to stand in as my mother to help me raise these babies."

"I hoped you'd want me." Cora's eyes were shiny with tears.

Michael couldn't swallow past the huge lump in his throat. He put his arms around both women, hugging them tightly. "Thanks, Mom."

He kissed her cheek, and Cora's eyes glowed.

"You're welcome, son."

IT TOOK only twenty minutes to get Bailey fixed up. The silk gown fit like a dream, the embroidered shoes like they'd been made for her.

"Thank goodness I had Brad to help me with the sizes," Cora muttered. She brushed Bailey's hair into a golden fall of brilliant sunshine. "Do you want your hair up?"

"Yes, please," Bailey said.

"No, thank you," Michael butted in.

"You're not even supposed to see the bride," Cora protested. "It's bad luck. You certainly don't get to choose her hairstyle."

"I don't believe in bad luck. I'm not letting Bailey out of my sight." Michael meant it. He'd nearly cried when he'd found Bailey gushing tears like rivers all over the place. Not one single soul besides his mother was going to even look at her unless he was at her side to protect her.

"Why don't you go get the cowboys?" Cora asked.

"What for?"

"Because I need one of them to drive your car around back. One of them can help me get Bailey into the car, and one can run go get your keys, change of clothes and the marriage certificate. If you go, half a dozen guests will stop you and want to talk."

A knock sounded at the door. They all three glanced at each other warily.

"Bailey, it's me," Brad said.

Instantly, Michael snatched open the door, pulled his soon-to-be brother-in-law through and locked it behind him.

"Bailey!" Brad cried.

"Sh!" they all told him.

"You're gorgeous!" He walked around his sister.

"Cora, you were right about the full skirt and the satin sash. It hides her stomach rather than bring focus to it."

"Brad, would you stop being an artist!" Bailey spread her hands wide. "Thank you for helping Cora with all of this. I feel like a fairy princess." She hugged him tightly.

"You are a princess, Bailey. I love you."

"I love you, too."

Michael couldn't wait any longer. "We've got an errand for you to run, if you don't mind helping, Brad."

"I'd love to.

"If you can round up three cowboys real fast," Michael said grimly, "we can get this show on the road and clear the property of all the guests. Mom's offered to help you with the kids, and I'm sure my cowboys would be eager for baby-sitting. My bride and I are going on a private wedding combination honeymoon."

Brad grinned hugely. "You'll be astonished at just how fast I can round up those crooked cowboys."

SUDDENLY, Bailey was being carefully secreted down a back stairway toward Michael's town car. White streamers had been tied to the antenna, and the door was open, waiting. She was ushered into the passenger seat, and Michael slid into the driver's seat. Quick kisses all around, even for the children, as Brad had sneaked them upstairs to say goodbye to their sister and Michael. In awe, they'd followed the procession down the staircase.

"Here," Fred said, thrusting a piece of paper through the window at Michael.

"What is it?" Michael carefully unfolded the paper, which had a dozen addresses and phone numbers on it.

"Wedding chapels in Vegas. I called information for ya. Wanted to make sure you reached the proper destination."

"Thanks, Fred." He tucked the paper safely into the suit jacket, which the cowboys had retrieved for him. "I guess I wasn't thinking of anything except getting there."

Fred nodded, his eyes on Bailey. "I owe it to Mr. and Mrs. Dixon to see that their daughter gets to the altar. You kids have fun—but no lollygagging on the way."

He stepped away from the car, and Chili smacked the trunk with his hand like he would a horse. "Go on with ya, now!"

"Are you ready?" Michael asked Bailey.

"I am."

He hesitated. "Bailey, there's something I have to tell you before we drive down this road. It's really important."

"What is it?"

He blew out a breath. "I was damn jealous of Gunner. And I'm always going to tell you how I feel about everything, so I hope you're prepared."

Her smile was luminous. "Oh, Michael. I'll drag the words out of your mouth with tweezers if I have to. I like hearing you tell me how much you love me."

"You won't have to. Every morning that I wake up, 'I love, you, Bailey,' are going to be the first words out of my mouth." He kissed her, and the flutters inside her told her that this was the beginning of all their happy days together.

"Let's drive off into the sunset, then," she said, when they finally pulled away from each other reluctantly.

"You got it." The car slowly moved forward down the lane. Her veil fluttering, Bailey leaned out the open window, waving at her guests. Everyone turned, and when they realized what was happening, they ran to the side of the road to call congratulations. Behind the car, Bailey could see Cora and the three cowboys waving goodbye. Brad was videotaping like mad with the video camera he'd borrowed from Deenie. The children ran behind the car, the lamb keeping up with Baby.

"Goodbye, Bailey!" Baby cried, waving wildly.

Bailey snatched up the corsage Deenie had given her and tossed the flowers to her youngest sister. Baby caught the flowers with delight.

"I'll be back soon!" Bailey called, blowing kisses. "You be good!"

"I will!" Baby called, blowing a kiss back with all her sisters and brothers doing the same.

"Stop!" Suddenly, Gunner was standing before the car to halt them. Everyone stopped clapping, tensely waiting to see what would happen.

Michael braked, looking out the open window at his rival suspiciously. Was this the final showdown between the two ranchers? All he knew was that he didn't want Bailey hurt or embarrassed in any way. If it meant swallowing his pride, he would do it gladly. "What is it, Gunner?"

"I just wanted you both to know I'm withdrawing my offer to the Dixon land and water rights." He grinned hugely. "I want to get along with my new neighbors."

Bailey and Michael smiled.

"Thanks, Gunner," Bailey said.

"I'd like to say the best man won, but maybe we both did," Gunner said to Michael.

"I think so. Thanks, Gunner."

"Have a good time." His rival stepped away, and the guests began cheering and clapping again as Michael drove to the end of the lane.

"You know," Michael said suddenly as they disappeared around the corner and were finally alone, "I'm going to like being part of your family."

Bailey snuggled up to his shoulder. "I'm going to like being part of yours."

He stopped the car right in the middle of the road. "I've got to kiss my bride."

And he did, until Bailey was breathless.

"I love you," he told her. "I always have. I just needed to stop being scared."

"I love you," she replied. "Someone who won't admit to being scared every once in a while isn't being honest. You're an honest man."

He kissed her. "I'm about to be, and darn glad you're making an honest man of me."

"I'm happy you're making an honest woman out of me," she said, her gaze steady and sure as she looked into his eyes. "You're all mine, cowboy."

SOME HOURS LATER they found just the right chapel. An elderly couple welcomed them, and Michael and Bailey became husband and wife in a touching ceremony that felt right to both of them.

Michael promised Bailey a romantic dinner for tomorrow night. Since they both needed their rest, they hurried to check into a fabulously neon-lit hotel, where the last thing they did was rest.

They were, after all, newlyweds.

Epilogue

When Bailey and Michael returned from Nevada, they had a small wedding ceremony at the church so that all the sisters and brothers could share their joy. The children were proud ringbearers and flower girls. Cora was the matron of honor, and Chili, Fred and Curly gave the bride away. Michael shot the garter at Brad, who caught it gladly—but there was an extra garter hidden on Bailey's thigh, which was just for Michael. And he made good on his promise to slowly remove that and all her clothes, as often as he could.

Bailey never hyphenated her name, after all. She decided she'd waited too long to be Mrs. Wade to hyphenate matters at this point. Somehow she never got around to opening a separate checking account, and before she knew it, she and all the children were living in Michael's house quite well. The lamb grew up and joined the other sheep, and Baby played outside with them the way she always had.

Not long after that, Bailey needed complete bed rest from the twins growing inside her. She often joked to Michael that she'd never been waited on hand and foot before, and that she might get used to it. Michael shook his head at her, telling her that a princess was supposed to be waited upon.

The ranch hands, including Fred, who reinstated himself at the Walking W, played the role of guardians to the Dixon children with great enthusiasm. They installed a gate between the two houses so that the children could run back and forth easily rather than having to climb over the fence.

Having the house to himself was an advantage to Brad. He saw his siblings constantly, but he could also see Deenie a lot, too, without much interruption. This led them to set a wedding date for the summer, after the babies were born, which was, coincidentally, about the same time Gunner decided he'd grown to like northern food and he'd just have to marry that Yankee gal. Since that Yankee gal had become great friends with Bailey and Deenie, the men put away their rivalry except for some good-hearted kidding about whose college team would win the most games, but that has ever been the case between the Aggies and the Longhorns, anyway.

Bailey thought her life had never been so happy, so full—until the day Doc Watson put two squirming bundles of joy on her stomach.

"A boy and a girl," Michael told her with pride. "I should have known you'd have a paired set. You always were a practical woman."

Bailey glowed as the children were pronounced healthy. Michael took her hand in his, leaning to give her a quick kiss.

"You came through that like a champion," she teased.

"What can I say?" he told her, his eyes alight with love. "I was made for this husband-father stuff."

"The real test is about to begin. Two o'clock, three o'clock, four o'clock wake-up calls."

He leaned close to whisper, "I was already keeping those hours with you."

Bailey laughed, and the nurses turned to see what she was laughing about. No one would ever know, though, exactly what made Michael and Bailey so happy.

The secret was, they loved each other. And they told each other and their children this—every day.

**Starting December 1999,
a brand-new series about
fatherhood from**

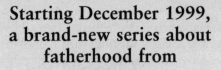

Three charming stories
about dads and kids...
and the women who
make their families
complete!

Available December 1999
FAMILY TO BE (#805)
by Linda Cajio

Available January 2000
A PREGNANCY AND A PROPOSAL (#809)
by Mindy Neff

Available February 2000
FOUR REASONS FOR FATHERHOOD (#813)
by Muriel Jensen

Available at your favorite retail outlet.

If you enjoyed what you just read,
then we've got an offer you can't resist!

Take 2 bestselling love stories FREE!

Plus get a FREE surprise gift!

Clip this page and mail it to Harlequin Reader Service®

IN U.S.A.
3010 Walden Ave.
P.O. Box 1867
Buffalo, N.Y. 14240-1867

IN CANADA
P.O. Box 609
Fort Erie, Ontario
L2A 5X3

YES! Please send me 2 free Harlequin American Romance® novels and my free surprise gift. Then send me 4 brand-new novels every month, which I will receive months before they're available in stores. In the U.S.A., bill me at the bargain price of $3.34 plus 25¢ delivery per book and applicable sales tax, if any*. In Canada, bill me at the bargain price of $3.71 plus 25¢ delivery per book and applicable taxes**. That's the complete price and a savings of over 10% off the cover prices—what a great deal! I understand that accepting the 2 free books and gift places me under no obligation ever to buy any books. I can always return a shipment and cancel at any time. Even if I never buy another book from Harlequin, the 2 free books and gift are mine to keep forever. So why not take us up on our invitation. You'll be glad you did!

154 HEN CNEX
354 HEN CNEY

Name _____ (PLEASE PRINT) _____

Address _____ Apt.# _____

City _____ State/Prov. _____ Zip/Postal Code _____

* Terms and prices subject to change without notice. Sales tax applicable in N.Y.
** Canadian residents will be charged applicable provincial taxes and GST.
    All orders subject to approval. Offer limited to one per household.
    ® are registered trademarks of Harlequin Enterprises Limited.

AMER99   ©1998 Harlequin Enterprises Limited

Back by popular demand are

DEBBIE
MACOMBER's

Hard Luck, Alaska, is a
town that needs women!
And the O'Halloran brothers
are just the fellows
to fly them in.

Starting in March 2000 this beloved series returns
in special 2-in-1 collector's editions:

MAIL-ORDER MARRIAGES, featuring
Brides for Brothers and *The Marriage Risk*
On sale March 2000

FAMILY MEN, featuring
Daddy's Little Helper and *Because of the Baby*
On sale July 2000

THE LAST TWO BACHELORS, featuring
Falling for Him and *Ending in Marriage*
On sale August 2000

Collect and enjoy each MIDNIGHT SONS story!

Available at your favorite retail outlet.

Come escape with Harlequin's new

Series Sampler

**Four great full-length Harlequin novels
bound together in one fabulous volume
and at an unbelievable price.**

Be transported back
in time with a
Harlequin Historical®
novel, get caught up
in a mystery with Intrigue®,
be tempted by a hot, sizzling romance
with Harlequin Temptation®,
or just enjoy a down-home
all-American read with
American Romance®.

You won't be able to put this collection down!

On sale February 2000 at your favorite retail outlet.

HARLEQUIN®
Makes any time special ™

Visit us at www.romance.net

PHESC